YOU JUST MIGHT GET IT

Behind Closed Doors Series Book 2

MONICA WALTERS

B. Love Publications

INTRODUCTION

Hello, Readers!

This is book two of the Behind Closed Doors Series. If you have not read book one, Be Careful What You Wish For, you will not fully understand what's going on in this book, since it continues where the first one left off.

This book also addresses mental health issues that could serve as triggers to readers. It contains steamy sex scenes, that include vulgar language. So, if any of these things might offend you, please do not read.

Thank you for purchasing and/or downloading this book. If you are okay with the previously mentioned warning, I hope that you enjoy the ride part two takes you on. It's getting crazy!

Monica

PROLOGUE

O mari

AFTER HELPING her in the car, I took a deep breath, thanking the good Lord for this woman. I had a lot I wanted to say to her, but I didn't know how. I'd fallen in love with her. My nerves kept me from just coming out and saying it, so I was trying to plan the right time to tell her. I decided that maybe I could say something today, after we left the movies or at dinner. Once I got in the car, we headed toward her parents' house to get Jordynn.

We'd ridden to school together, today, since our final exams were at the same time. As I drove, my mind kept trying to plan how and when I would say it. Then, I started thinking, what if she doesn't say it back? In my heart, I believed she loved me, too, so I would just take the chance. I'd cross that bridge when I got to it. "Why are you so quiet, baby? You thinking about baby girl, huh?"

"Yeah," I said quietly.

"She's gonna be fine, if Piper gets her shit together and wants to see her. And you will be, too."

"I hope you're right."

After getting to her mama's house, I noticed a car in the driveway. We both looked at one another, not knowing who the car was for and shrugged our shoulders. When we walked in the house, Ashahve's hand flew to her mouth and I frowned deeply. "What in the hell are you doing here?"

"I came back for my daughter..."

1

O mari

"COME OUTSIDE, Piper. I refuse to disrespect the Glasper's house."

I grabbed her arm, halfway pulling her ass out the door. Jordynn was sitting there with the biggest smile on her face, happy to see her mama. Once we got outside, I could see Ashahve watching us from the door. My face was twitching uncontrollably. I was so fucking mad. "What the fuck wrong wit'chu? You not gon' keep making these changes in my baby's life. She's fine just where she is."

"Rich, for real? I did that to teach yo' ass a lesson."

I frowned at her ass and was ready to grab her by the damn neck. "What the fuck you talking about? You act like I wasn't taking care of my daughter. I gave your ass three hundred dollars, every two weeks and I bought shit for my baby every chance I got. Not to mention, I spend as much time with her as I can, so get the fuck outta here with that bullshit, Piper. You back on that ratchet shit, I see, but I ain't gon' stand for that fuck-shit this time."

"I needed to show you how it felt to be left alone with a child to raise. After all that time I put up with your fucking attitudes, your mood swings and depression, you had the nerve to not want me after that. I stuck around through all that bullshit! Then, when you got yourself together, I was no longer good enough for you. I straightened my life up, started going to school, became a better mother and provider for Tutu, and tried to leave the hood behind. I did that shit for you, Rich! For you!"

"That's the problem. You should've done that shit for yourself! Don't make it seem like you were a damn saint when I was going through my issues. You fucking cheated on me... several times. Why would I hang around for that shit? Huh?" I pushed her with my fingertips. "Answer me! You done came to my girl's parents' house with this shit. How the fuck do you know where they live anyway?"

"I followed Ashahve from school yesterday. I needed to know where my baby was."

"Bitch, you have my phone number! You never once called to even see how Jordynn was doing. Miss me on that. Now, you need to leave before I call the police! If I don't call them, I'm liable to beat yo' ass! Get on!"

I walked away from her as she yelled my name and screamed, "This shit ain't over!"

When I turned and scowled at her, she quickly got in her car. There was a better way for her to do the shit she did. If she needed a fucking break, that was all she had to say, instead of dramatizing this shit the way she did. As I walked in the house, I noticed Mrs. Glasper and Jordynn weren't in the front room anymore, but Ashahve was sitting on the couch.

I joined her on the sofa and pulled her hand in mine. "I'm sorry, baby. I know this shit irritates you. I'm going talk to a lawyer tomorrow to see what I can do about Piper. I don't mind Jordynn seeing Piper, but this ain't no fucking revolving door. She not gon' treat my baby like that."

"Omari, I understand you're angry, but please watch your

language. My mama and Jordynn are in the next room. There's no reason for an apology. We just have to do what we have to do."

"I'm sorry. I'm just so pissed, I could have choked the fuck out of her," I said in a lower tone. After taking a deep breath, I said, "I wanted to take the two of you to dinner tonight. Is that still feasible?"

After this shit, the movies were out. We wouldn't have time for me to calm down, so it would be a waste of money, because I wouldn't enjoy the shit.

"Let me think on it, okay?"

"Aight. Let me get Jordynn, so we can go home and change, and I can try to do something with her hair."

"My mama is braiding her hair now."

"Okay," I said as I leaned back on the cushions of the sofa. "Are you angry with me?"

"No, just at the situation."

How could I have prevented this from happening? There was nothing I could have done. I hoped she realized that. It didn't seem she did, though. I had big plans. I wanted to tell her I was in love with her tonight. This time of year was extra significant, too. My mama's birthday was tomorrow. Because of Ashahve, I didn't feel as torn up about it as I normally did. But I could see, now, that I needed to take a trip to the cemetery, especially if she didn't wanna go to dinner tonight.

We sat there in silence for a moment, then Ashahve grabbed my hand. "If you're wondering... I'm not losing you without a fight. I just need a minute to process what's going on and how I'm gonna handle it. This past month, with you, has been amazing."

She moved her hand to my beard and gently rubbed her fingers through it. That gesture had calmed me down significantly and damn, it was turning me on. "So, how you wanna handle it?"

"I *wanna* beat her ass for hopping in and out of baby girl's life. That's why I have to come up with something else. I can't stoop to her level. My mama didn't raise me that way."

I leaned over to her and kissed those pretty lips. Relief flooded my being as we kissed. Shawty was gon' be me and Jordynn's ride or die. I could feel that shit. Well, as long as I didn't fuck up, she would be. I had no intentions of doing that, though. When I pulled away from her, I noticed her cheeks were rosy. I gave her a one-cheeked smile. "You know, you can always come with us. When Jordynn takes a nap, I can give you what'chu want."

She gave me a slight smile, then kissed me again. "Sounds like a plan, big daddy."

My eyebrows lifted and I lowered my head while keeping my eyes on her. "Oh, I'm big daddy?"

"Nope. He is," she said, looking at my rising erection.

I chuckled. "You better cut that shit out before I take you to my car."

Before she could respond, Jordynn and Mrs. Glasper came from the back room. "Da-dy! Look!"

Jordynn twirled so I could see her hair. It was in several cornrows and there was a bow at the back where they all came together. "Wow, munchkin! That looks so beautiful. Did you tell Na-Na thank you?"

She ran back to Mrs. Glasper and hugged her tightly. "Thank you, Na-Na."

I smiled, then looked to Mrs. Glasper. "I'm so sorry."

"It's okay. I understand, and I hope you two can figure something out."

"Da-dy? Where did Mama go?"

I exhaled and closed my eyes for a second, then kneeled in front of her. "We'll talk about that in the car. Okay, baby?"

"Okaaayy," she said sadly.

I picked her up as I stood and Ashahve stood as well. "You coming with us?"

"No, baby. I better not. I'm gonna chill out for a minute with my mama and spend some time with my daddy when he gets home. Y'all can pick me up for dinner. How should I dress?"

"We're gonna go to Floyd's, if you feeling that."

"That's cool, baby. What time should I be ready?"

"Is seven too soon?"

"No, it's perfect."

Ashahve kissed my lips, then Jordynn's cheek as she giggled, then followed us out. When I walked out the door, I could have fucked somebody up. My car was on a flat. I knew that bitch did that shit. Piper wasn't gon' stop until it was too late. I sat baby girl on her feet and rubbed my hand over the top of my head. Anger was trying to consume me, on some real shit. I got my spare from the trunk and changed the tire as Ashahve and Jordynn watched. "Da-dy, what happened?"

"He has a flat tire, baby girl," I heard Ashahve say to her.

The whole time I was loosening the lugs, I was imagining myself punching Piper in her shit and going to jail. Thoughts of fucking a woman up had never embodied me this strong. Overseas, I'd killed women and children without batting an eye and that shit desensitized me tremendously, but I'd been successful at pushing it to the back of my mind. Piper was bringing that shit to the forefront again.

I didn't want any problems with keeping my baby, so I was gonna have to talk to somebody before I lost control on Piper's ass. My last stint in Iraq, I'd shot a kid. It was a good thing I did, though, because he was the one that shot me in the leg. Had I not done it, he would've killed me. It didn't stop that shit from bothering me, though. I went through counseling for months after that, and I thought I was cool with it, until today.

Once I'd jacked the car up and changed the tire, I called for baby girl to come get in the car. We were gonna have to take a trip to my job to buy another one. That bitch slashed the fuck out of that tire. There was no saving that shit. Piper wasn't gon' ruin the rest of my day, though. After I got a new tire, Jordynn and I were gonna go to my mama's gravesite for a little bit, then go home and clean up.

Ashahve walked over to me and grabbed my trembling hand. "I know this is hard. But you have two reasons to keep it together: that little angel right there and the angel in front of you."

I smirked. "I don't know about the one standing in front of me.

You might be a fallen angel, cause ain't shit angelic about what you do to me in the bedroom."

She rolled her eyes and laughed as I laughed along with her. "Well, at least you can make jokes. Seriously, I need you to stay focused on Jordynn and what's best for her, no matter what Piper does. Okay?"

She put her hands in my beard again and I closed my eyes. When I opened them, I laid my lips on hers. "I got'chu, baby."

2

A shahve

IT LITERALLY FELT like I was pulling Omari off the ledge. He was so angry, and he definitely had reason to be. Everything in me wanted to snatch Piper off my mama's sofa when I saw her sitting there with Jordynn. That bitch had some nerve to show up at *my* parents' house. I was so glad Omari took her outside to argue with her. Watching them from the storm door, I wanted to interfere so badly. His face was as red as a damn fire engine. That was why I had to make sure he didn't cross the line.

After he and Jordynn left, I sat and thought about the situation. While he was angry, I could also see how hurt he was. This past month, we'd gotten used to Jordynn being around all the time. I just prayed she didn't start acting out because of her confusion about why she couldn't go with her mama. As I sat there, kind of awkwardly staring off into space, my mama sat next to me. She grabbed my hand and said, "This is a delicate mess."

I frowned slightly, but then I realized what she meant. "Yeah, it is. I hope Omari's able to explain it to Jordynn in a way that makes sense in her mind."

"Yeah. She was so excited when she saw her mama through the storm door. There was no way I could've turned the girl around after that. Was she and Omari ever a couple?"

"Yes, ma'am. I think they broke up when Jordynn was a year old. She was so cool when I first met her, but it was like a switch went off when she realized how serious Omari was about me."

"He loves you. I can see it, plain as day. Has he told you yet?"

"No, ma'am." I turned facing my mama. My heart was full. "I'm in love with him, Mama. I'm afraid to tell him, though, because I want him to say it back. I feel like he loves me, but when it comes to matters of the heart, Omari can be so shut off at times."

"What does he do to make you feel like he loves you?"

"Well..." I started. I couldn't tell her everything. My mama and I never talked about sex. "The way he looks at me, it's like he's staring through to my soul. When he talks to me, it's like he's communing with my spirit. Even when he makes me laugh, he has my mind baffled with how he can come up with punch lines so quickly. Everything about him has me in awe and I know it has to be the same for him."

"Wow, baby."

I couldn't tell her that even when he's angry, it turns me on. It makes me think about our rough sex sessions. The way he takes control of my body, making it submit to him, is nothing short of amazing. Everything about him turns me on, not to mention his relationship with his baby. My mama grabbed my hand. "I'm so happy you have a man that does all that for you. That makes you feel like you're special. Every good parent wants their children to be happy, and I can truly see you're happy."

I leaned against her as my dad walked through the door. He was retired, but still went to work every day. I didn't understand it. When I retired, that would be it. I'd start traveling more and enjoying the fruits of my labor. Daddy didn't stay all day, but he would go about ten in the morning and come home close to three. "Hey, y'all!" he said excitedly. "I'm surprised you're here, Shavi."

I playfully rolled my eyes, then stood from my seat to greet Michael Glasper. My daddy was the old school, provider type husband, where his wife didn't have to hit a lick at a stick. They were up in age when they met and got married. My dad was almost forty when they had me and forty-three when my brother came along. My mama was ten years younger than him, which was why it was so easy for me to be infatuated with Dr. Coleman.

"Well, Daddy, I thought that I could spend time with the two of you today."

"Well, I'll say. I'm sixty-two years old and I don't think I've ever heard you or June say that you wanted to spend time with me."

June was my brother. His name was Michael Glasper, Jr., so, to differentiate the two from one another, everyone called my brother June. "I'm sorry, Daddy. That's gonna be changing. At least for me anyway. Maybe after June graduates, later this month, he'll be more apt to spend time with you as well."

"Okay. Okay. Where's my little munchkin? She usually comes running to the door."

"Omari's off today. You actually just missed them, about thirty minutes ago. Along with Jordynn's mother."

His eyebrows rose. "Yeah. That was my exact reaction, too," I added.

"I know Omari didn't handle that too well. I noticed that he can have a temper. He hasn't been like that with you, has he?"

"No, sir. Omari has never disrespected me, but he does have a temper at times, and I think it has a lot to do with his days in the military and the loss of his mother. Honestly, I still don't think he's done grieving."

"Has he thought about seeking counseling?" my mama asked.

"We don't really talk about it much. That's why I think it's still hard for him. Whenever I ask a question about his mom, he answers it, but then changes the subject. He never knew his dad, so his mama was all he had. But the way he loves baby girl brings joy to my soul. I've never seen him get angry with her, even when she's cutting up. He's so patient with her. It's like she puts his soul at ease, and I'm beginning to see that I do that for him as well."

My daddy gave me a soft smile. "He seems like a good guy, Shavi. Just don't move too fast. Take your time and really get to know him. Okay?"

"I will, Daddy. Thank you."

We sat around, talking for another hour or so when my brother walked in. He spoke, then went to his room as my dad slowly shook his head. I chuckled, then went to my room to start getting ready for dinner with Omari and Jordynn, as my mom went to the kitchen to start warming their dinner. After talking to my mama about how I felt about Omari, I was glad that I agreed to go to dinner, despite how I felt about the whole situation with Piper.

It made me wonder if he'd led her on in any way before we got together, making her think that they had a chance. Even if that were the case, he was mine now and she needed to respect that. Neither Jordynn nor I had shit to do with whatever it was she was feeling for Omari. Furthermore, whatever she was feeling for Omari she could keep to herself. He'd told her that on several occasions.

After primping in the mirror, admiring my size eight frame and ass in my tight, mid-thigh-length dress, I headed to the front room to wait for Omari. "Where you going in that?"

I frowned as I turned to look at my eighteen-year-old brother. "June, the last time I checked, I was grown. Even before that, I ain't neva had to answer to yo' ass."

"Whateva. You look nice," he said, then kissed my head.

I smirked at him. "Thank you."

When I got to the front room, there was a knock on the door. My mama looked me up and down, then said, "Well, damn. Don't y'all make me no grandbabies tonight."

My face had to be red, because it was hot as hell. I couldn't believe she'd said that. I went to the door and opened it to see Omari in some slacks and a nice dress shirt and Jordynn in a cute, little pink dress. They were both holding flowers. It was the cutest thing ever. As I opened the door, I watched Omari's eyes scan my body and his long, thick tongue lick his lips.

"Hi, Shavi! These are for you!" Jordynn said excitedly.

I supposed their talk had gone well, since Jordynn was in a good mood. "Thank you, baby!"

I took them from her and kissed her cheek as she walked in the house. "Papa!" she yelled as I stared at Omari.

I was at a loss for words at just how good he looked in those black slacks and white shirt. Damn, he was so fine. "Ya man clean up good, right?"

I nodded slowly as I stared at him. He laughed and it broke me out of the trance he clearly had me in. Pulling me closer to him, he said in my ear, "You look beautiful, baby. Now, quit looking at me like that before I ask your parents if Jordynn can stay with them."

I gently bit his earlobe, then pulled away from him. He could play if he wanted to, but I could play better. The smirk on his lips said that he knew that shit, too. "Omari, you look nice," my mama said.

I turned to see her standing behind me and daddy next to her, holding Jordynn in his arms. "Thank you, Mrs. Glasper."

His eyes landed on mine again, and said, "Don't plan on coming home tonight, shawty."

My face heated up, along with other places on my body, as I stared at him. "Da-dy, can Na-Na and Papa come, too?"

"Maybe next time, baby girl."

I took my flowers from him to put them in water, then we headed out.

Once we got to Floyd's, Omari seemed extremely quiet. We'd talked briefly about how he told Jordynn that he and Piper needed to talk before she could see her again. He said Jordynn seemed to understand. As long as she would get to eventually see Piper, she was okay.

Hopefully, they worked this out soon, for her sake. He walked around and opened my door, then Jordynn's.

"Thank you, Da-dy."

"Yeah. Thank you, Daddy."

Jordynn giggled as Omari looked at me with a one-cheeked smile on his face. Instead of allowing Jordynn to walk between us, he walked in the middle, holding me at my waist. He kissed my shoulder. "Damn, shawty. You look so good. I can't wait to hear you call me daddy later," he mumbled close to my ear.

"I bet you can't."

He chuckled as we walked inside. Being that it was a weekday, we were seated right away. You couldn't get within a mile of this place on the weekends. Their food was that good. They sold a variety of seafood and American cuisine that kept people in southeast Texas feeling right at home. The atmosphere was light, and it was just an all-around comfortable setting.

"Ooooh, I want some alligator," I said as I salivated merely at the thought.

"Alligator?" Jordynn asked with her face scrunched up.

Omari chuckled. "Yeah, baby girl. They cut the tail up in pieces and fry it."

"Yuck!"

We both laughed at Jordynn's facial expression. The waitress came to take our drink and appetizer orders, and we were practically quiet until she returned. I was known to lack conversation, at times, but lately, I'd feed off Omari. But he was quiet. Before we could dig into the alligator, Omari grabbed my hand. My eyes lifted to his and he grabbed Jordynn's as well. I could feel the slight tremble in his hand, and it made me somewhat nervous.

Omari didn't seem to have a fearful bone in his body, but here he was trembling like he was scared. He bowed his head and began to pray. That was odd as well, because we always said our own grace. I listened to him thank the Lord for the food and for us being able to dine together. Then he said, "I also wanna thank you for bringing

Ashahve into our lives. She's the woman I've always wanted. I hope she can feel how much I love her, because I suck at this emotional thing."

My eyes popped open and I stared at him as he continued. "Lord, she's perfect for me. Help me to give her everything she desires emotionally... everything she needs. In Jesus name, Amen."

The tears were falling down my cheeks as Omari opened his eyes and looked right at me. "I love you, Ashahve."

I felt like I was hyperventilating. I always thought I would be the one to say it first, without knowing for sure if I'd get a response. "I love you, too, Shavi!" Jordynn added.

I swallowed hard and stood to my feet as he watched. After walking over to him, he stood from his seat and I pulled his face to mine and laid a huge kiss on him. "Omari, I love you, too."

The tears really sprang from my eyes, just from saying those words to him. He pulled me in his arms and held me close, as Jordynn asked, "What's wrong?"

Pulling away from him, I turned to her and said, "I love you, too, baby. And, for once, nothing's wrong. Everything is right."

❄ 3 ❄

O mari

I WAS nervous as hell when I finished praying and saw the tears on Ashahve's face. My heart felt like it stopped beating for a minute. I was *so* damn nervous until I was nauseated and now, she was sitting here crying. But the moment she said I love you, too, all was right in my world. We were in love and I couldn't be happier. When she sat back in her seat, she kept her eyes on mine and I could see the sincerity in them. That shit was so overwhelming, I had to look away.

I gave Jordynn a piece of alligator dipped in ketchup and winked at Ashahve. Jordynn plopped it in her mouth, no questions asked. I glanced back at Ashahve and she was watching Jordynn. "Is it good, Jordynn?" Ashahve asked.

"It's a little pepper. It's good, too!"

I couldn't hide the smile on my face. Just as I was about to tell her that it was alligator, Shavi interrupted me by saying, "You will not."

I laughed, feeling the best I've ever felt, in a long time, in my mother's birthday month. After leaving the Glasper's and going to my job to buy a tire, Jordynn and I went home instead of going to the cemetery. I was too angry, and I didn't want to get emotional in front of my baby. She would have been scared if she would have seen me cry. Plus, I wanted Ashahve to be with me, the next time I went.

"Omari?"

"Yeah?"

I stretched my arms across the table, and she put her hands in mine. "Was the whole purpose of this dinner to tell me you love me?"

"No. The whole purpose was to eat some good food and get full."

She rolled her eyes as I laughed. I continued, truthfully. "Yeah, it was. I wanted to take you somewhere nice, before I bore my soul to you. It feels good to be able to say it now. I love you, girl."

"I love you, too. I've been feeling this way for the past week and I thought I would be the first one to say it."

"Shocked you, huh?"

"Shocked isn't the word," she said, then giggled.

"Da-dy, can I have some more chicken?"

I fought to hold in my smile. "Sure, baby girl."

I put her three pieces on a plate with some ketchup and slid it in front of her as she licked her lips. I chuckled as Ashahve desperately tried to hold in her laughter. The waitress returned to our table to take our orders, then smiled at Jordynn. "Aww, she loves the..."

"Chicken! She loves the chicken," Ashahve yelled.

I laughed, unable to hold it in any longer. The waitress joined me after she realized why Ashahve cut her off. "You two have an adorable daughter."

"Aww, thanks, but..."

"Thank you," I said, nodding at the waitress.

Ashahve blushed as I grabbed her hand and leaned over to kiss it. Despite what Piper had done earlier, to try to ruin our day, tonight was perfect. Or so I thought, until Ashahve's gaze drifted to whomever was behind me. Before I could turn around, her eyes had landed back on mine and her face was a little red. "Shaviiii!"

A woman ran up to her and practically yanked her from her seat. My eyebrows rose out of curiosity. "Hey, Nyera! What are you doing in town?"

"I gotta job at Lamar as an A&P instructor! When I went to visit your parents, the other day, you weren't there."

Before Ashahve could introduce her, I figured out why her face was red. Dr. Coleman was standing behind whoever this woman was to her. His face was red as hell, too. I didn't know if it was just the awkwardness of the situation or what. He and I had never met face to face this way. Before I could address him, Ashahve said, "Omari, this is my cousin, Nyera. Her mama and my mama are sisters. Nyera, this is my boyfriend, Omari and his daughter, Jordynn."

I nodded, then shook her outstretched hand. She made her way to Jordynn and shook her hand as well, while Jordynn giggled. When Nyera stepped back over to her 'date' for the night, she said, "I'm not sure if you know my date or not, but this is Dr. Coleman. He's a sociology professor at Lamar and agreed to show me around town."

"I've had a few of his classes. Hello, Dr. Coleman."

"Hello, Ms. Glasper. How are you?"

"I'm great. This is my boyfriend, Omari Watson. Omari, this is Dr. Coleman."

It took everything in me to actually reach out and shake his hand. *Chill out, Rich. You got the girl. She loves you.* Even with my subconscious speaking to me, reminding me of where I stood in Ashahve's life, I also knew that he loved her, too. "Nice to meet you, Mr. Watson."

Is it? Had I not been in Ashahve's life, they would probably be together. I only nodded in response and, at that moment, I think he realized that I knew about their past. Ashahve and her cousin started to catch up as he and I stood there silently. I watched him try to look at anything in the restaurant besides Ashahve. After taking a deep breath, he said, "Your daughter is beautiful."

"Thank you."

I nodded and swallowed hard as I sat, then gestured for him to have a seat on the other side of Jordynn. It didn't look like Nyera and Ashahve would be wrapping up their conversation anytime soon. When the waitress passed our table, I got her attention to order a Henny and Coke. "Hi. My name is Jordynn," I heard my baby say to Dr. Coleman.

"Nice to meet you. I'm Elijah."

He shook her hand and she giggled. "Why do adults shake hands?"

I shook my head slowly, then smiled. "It's just a way we greet."

She shrugged her shoulders as Dr. Coleman smiled at her. "I'm sorry, Elijah. I hadn't seen my cousin in years, and I got excited. Are you ready to go to our table?" Nyera said to him.

"Yes. Again, nice meeting you, Mr. Watson and Miss Jordynn. Nice seeing you again, Ms. Glasper."

He shook my hand and Jordynn's, then nodded at Ashahve. When they walked away, she slowly exhaled, then reached for my hand. "I'm sorry."

"He's in the past. I'm cool. I take it we may be seeing more of him, since he's with your cousin."

"Possibly. They aren't a couple. They just met earlier today, on campus."

I nodded and drank my Henny while Jordynn worked on her French fries. We enjoyed the rest of our dinner, sharing our entrees and feeding one another, still basking in our newly revealed love for one another. After paying for our meal and leaving a tip, we left. Once we got to the car, Jordynn said, "Da-dy, I'm full."

"That's good, baby. You ate a lot."

"It was good!"

I chuckled, then opened Ashahve's door. "Somebody will be sleeping before we get home."

She licked her lips, then bit her bottom one before getting in the car. I winked at her as I felt my dick hardening. I closed her door, then strapped my baby in her car seat. As I walked around the car, I saw Dr. Coleman and Nyera heading to their ride, but I quickly turned my head, so I didn't have to acknowledge them. I didn't have anything against Ashahve's cousin, but I wasn't trying to be chummy with a man she used to fuck not so long ago.

Once I'd gotten in the car, I saw Ashahve's cousin waving. We both waved back before I started the engine and left out of the parking lot. "You have to work tomorrow, baby?"

"No."

"You wanna come with me to get Jordynn registered for school?"

"Of course."

Ashahve glanced at the backseat to see Jordynn was already out, then looked back at me. "What do you plan to do about Piper?"

"Honestly, shawty, I don't know. While I don't want Jordynn spending time with a woman that didn't care to check on her for a whole month, what can I do about it? Even if the courts award me custody, they won't forbid her from seeing Jordynn."

"Do you actually want that?"

"I want her to see Jordynn, but I don't want overnight visits. I just question her motives now. I could never go a month without seeing or talking to my baby by choice."

"I suppose I understand, baby. I don't have kids, but I still don't understand how she did that shit."

"Enough about that shit, shawty. I need you to concentrate on how I'm gon' make love to that body tonight."

I mainly changed the subject for me. Thinking about Piper was only gonna piss me off. When I was angry, I fucked. I wanted to give Ashahve my soft side tonight, showing her how it felt to have my heart. It wasn't that I'd been holding back... well, I guess I had been. Love wasn't easy for me to accept, especially since my mama had been gone. However, having ratchet ass females around all the time, it was easy to keep those feelings tucked away. The ones I dealt with, thought that sex would soften a nigga.

They weren't really my type. That was why I fucked around with them to begin with. The sex was mostly good as hell, but that was it. There was no serious conversation, no talks of dreams and aspirations, or talks about family. A woman like Ashahve, one that was driven to do something more with their life, was what I wanted. She wasn't waiting on a man to rescue her. I loved that about her. Of course, she was fine as hell while doing it. She had a calm spirit that could easily calm me, like my mama.

"How you gon' make love to me tonight that's any different than what you've been doing, Omari?"

"Oh, so you doubting yo' man, shawty? You gon' see."

She giggled, then grabbed my hand. "I'm not doubting you, baby. I just thought you'd *been* making love to me."

"Oh, yeah, li'l mama? Well, brace yourself, baby."

"Well, ain't that some shit. You been holding out on me. You better unleash all that shit tonight."

I laughed as a smile played at her lips. "I can't just unleash everything. Jordynn gon' wake up with all the screaming you would be doing. Can't be tainting my baby's ears."

"Uh huh. Whatever, Omari," she said while laughing.

Ashahve's phone chimed, alerting her of a text. After I saw her face turn slightly red, I knew it was probably that nigga. I just hoped I didn't have to break that dude's neck. I'd unleash all this street and military training on his ass. As she typed a response, I saw her glance at me. "What'd he say?"

Her eyes widened, like she didn't think I knew it was him. Ashahve only had one friend that really texted her a lot. Other than that, her phone didn't ring too often. "He was apologizing for being with my cousin, and if I wanted him to back off, he would."

"He obviously didn't know y'all were kin."

"No. I accepted his apology, but I don't know what to say. It doesn't bother me if he talks to her, I just don't wanna see him at my parents' house... ever. I don't want him around you. I don't want you to feel some type of way if she brings him around. Hell, I don't wanna be uncomfortable either. There would be no way around that without telling Nyera what he and I once shared."

"I don't know, Shavi. It would be extremely uncomfortable, and I wouldn't wanna have to gouge that nigga eyes out for looking at you too long."

She slid her hands down her face and exhaled hard. She was obviously bothered by seeing him. I just hoped it wasn't because she still felt something for him. "Don't worry about that shit, right now, shawty. You don't even know if your cousin will continue to see him. Chill out."

"You're right. I won't answer his question."

I grabbed her hand and brought it to my lips, then intertwined my fingers with hers. Her heart was so big and that was one of the things I admired about her. I just didn't want his ass to reap the benefits of that. When we got to my apartment, I opened Shavi's door, then scooped Jordynn up from her car seat. Li'l mama was knocked out. Her braids flung to the side as I lifted her, causing her to lay her head on my shoulder.

"She's out," Shavi said and giggled.

"Yep. She ate herself into that good, comatose sleep."

Jordynn took a deep breath and moaned as we walked to the apartment, causing us to laugh. Before we could get to the door, she was talking in her sleep. "Da-dy, look at me. I'm skating," she said a little above a whisper.

It was taking everything in us to only laugh at her quietly. She was so cute, though. As I unlocked the door, Shavi rubbed her hair and kissed her forehead. I couldn't imagine life without my little brown-eyed princess. And now that she was living with me, Piper was gon' catch hell tryna get her back. I didn't trust her to take care of her anymore. If she could turn her back on my baby that easily, what would keep her from doing it again?

I brought Jordynn to her bedroom, with Shavi right behind me. We worked together to take her clothes off, as easily as possible so we wouldn't wake her. Jordynn began talking again, but this time, it warmed our hearts. "I love you, Shavi. Da-dy love you, too."

"I'm glad I told you that earlier. Jordynn telling all the best kept secrets in her sleep."

Shavi laughed quietly as I covered my baby with her Moana comforter. We quietly left her room and closed the door as her lamp spun slowly, illuminating the ceiling with stars. Pulling Shavi close to me, I kissed her forehead and circled my arms around her. "It feels good to tell you that I love you. I've been holding it in for at least a month now."

"I know what you mean. I love you, too, Omari."

I scooped her in my arms and kissed her lips as I headed to my bedroom with her. Despite all the bullshit that had happened today, I needed to make love to her. I needed her to feel how deeply I felt for her. She was in my soul and that had been an impossible feat that she'd conquered without even knowing it.

Once inside, I gently laid her on the bed, then locked the door. Turning back to her, she was lying there with her legs bent, feet flat on the bed. I could see her thong and it was soaked in her juices. I slowly licked my lips, then made my way to her. After pulling my shirt over my head, I slid between her legs like a baseball player sliding into home plate.

I ripped her silk and lace thong right off her, and dove tongue-first into her. Shavi flinched at my roughness and let a moan escape her lips. She was so sweet and was her own flavor of Kool-Aid. I loved Kool-Aid. Swirling my tongue around her trigger, she grabbed my head and pulled me closer, practically drowning me in that mango squeeze. Once I began sucking her clit, I slid two fingers inside of her and held her in place with my other arm.

She was squirming all over the bed, moaning softly, while her hands held my head in place. I hit that G-spot in the come hither motion, as I sucked her clit. She removed her hands from my head, then grabbed a pillow and screamed into it as she came all over my face. I literally had to stop before she drowned me. She was squirting everywhere, and I loved every minute of it. I couldn't wait for her to stop.

I wanted her to squirt on me where it counted most. Swiftly removing my pants, I dove into her pussy as she continued to release her juices. Staying on my knees, as I lifted her hips and stroked her slowly, I watched that thang juice all over my dick. That shit had me trembling. I was so damned turned on and turned out, I could feel my nut rising already.

It was too soon for that shit. My lil baby deserved an all-night worship of her body. That body was just as blessed as her heart. It was what first attracted me to her. That coke bottle ain't had shit on Shavi. Her ass was like two fluffy pillows that made a nigga weak and she had the thighs to match that shit.

She removed the pillow from her face as I released her hips and leaned over her, tongue kissing those Hershey kisses on her chest. I swore her nipples had chocolate coming from them. Everything about her body had me addicted... craving her daily. Shit, if I could have her every hour, I would. Her soft moans were like music to my ears, serenading me through this amazing workout. Not to mention the accompaniment her pussy was giving. That made it a masterpiece that I should be recording.

Those gushy noises were like balm to an open wound... healing me in every way imaginable. My lips made their way to hers and I kissed her like my life depended on it. She was the nourishment to my heart... my soul... my mind, and this was the only way I felt completely comfortable saying that to her. I said it through my actions, and by the sounds she was making, I had no choice but to assume she was pleased.

When I pulled my lips from hers, I stared in her eyes as they widened from the intensity of our love making. I was stroking her slow, but deep. I bit my bottom lip as her warm wetness covered my shaft and balls. Her legs trembled and her nails scratched my back. I whispered in her ear after kissing her neck, "I love you, girl."

"Ahhh... I love you, too, Omari."

Gently biting her earlobe, I pushed even deeper, as she wrapped her legs around my waist, giving me unlimited access to her depths. I grabbed her thigh and held her leg up in the air, kissing behind her knees, as I continued to stroke her perfection. I mentally thanked

God for making her just for me, 'cause that's what it felt like. Like He specifically made every part of her to please me. And whatever God makes for you is tailored to fit you perfectly. That's what I felt about my Ashahve.

"Omari... shit! This love feels so gooooood."

I watched the tears fall down her cheeks and I did my best to kiss every one of them. I spread her legs, then grabbed the backs of her knees and pushed them to her head. As I dipped in her goodness repeatedly, she began pulling her hair. "Damn, shawty. This love is the shit, for real, baby."

I leaned over her, letting her legs rest on my shoulders and continued to make love to the woman I wanted to be mine forever. Before long, our quiet grunts and moans, became louder and more passionate, filling the room with the intensity of our love. "Shavi, fuck! I'm 'bout to let you have this shit."

"Yeeeess, baby. Give it to me. I'm about to give it to you again!"

This would be her third time. The growls leaving my throat as I plowed into her made me sound like a mad man. That was okay, though, 'cause her shit was taking me down... fast. I let my head drop to the pillow as my seed filled her. She wrapped her legs around me, once again, squeezing me tightly as her orgasm coursed through her body. I could stay buried here forever. "I love you, Shavi."

"I love you, too."

🌟 4 🌟

E lijah

WHEN I SAW Ashahve in Floyd's, I could have disappeared. That was my first time being in her presence when she was with her boyfriend. They looked so happy, and I discreetly watched them all night. The fact that I was there with her cousin took me by surprise completely. While Nyera was intelligent, beautiful and fine as hell, my heart still held Ashahve in it. I believed Omari saw that in my eyes. That also let me know that he knew about us. He was cordial, though, so I relaxed a little and focused my attention on his little princess.

I was shocked that Nyera had wanted to go out so soon. Honestly, I didn't expect her to even call as soon as she did. I was supposed to call her. She was a gorgeous woman; beautiful skin, the color of almonds, but smooth like butter, pouty lips and slanted brown eyes. The twists in her hair were gorgeous and a complete turn on for me.

She was passionate about teaching, just like I was, and most of our initial conversation was about the university.

After we left and I'd brought her home, I knew quite a bit about her. She had two brothers and a sister and had been in Longview all her life. Most times, when she'd seen Ashahve was when they made trips to Longview or other family locations. Ashahve and her immediate family were the only ones living in Beaumont. Her mom's family was from Longview. Nyera had never been married but had been engaged before, like me, and didn't have any children.

We had a lot in common and I was looking forward to getting to know her. So, when Ashahve never really responded to whether or not she would be okay with me dating Nyera, I got a little nervous. She accepted my apology, so I knew she'd seen the second part of the text about if she wanted me to back off. I would never want to make her uncomfortable. I missed her, but I knew that I had to move on. It just so happened that I moved on to her cousin.

Life could be so cruel, at times. Since she didn't respond to that part of the text, I had to assume it was okay. My phone rang, breaking me from my thoughts. When I picked it up, I saw it was Nyera. "Hello?"

"Hi, Elijah. I just wanted to say, again, how much I enjoyed your company tonight. Thank you so much."

"I enjoyed you, too, Nyera. You're an amazing person. You wanna hang tomorrow?"

"Thank you. So are you! I would love to hang out tomorrow."

I smiled. "Well, think about something you may wanna do and let me know. I'm open to whatever."

"Can I cook for you?"

My eyebrows had risen. "You wanna cook for me?"

"Yes. I can cook. Don't worry."

I chuckled. "I'm not worried about that."

"Well, what *are* you worried about?"

"I'd rather talk to you face to face about it. So, will you cook at your place or mine?"

"You probably have a bigger kitchen and I have stuff everywhere. So, can I come there?"

"Of course."

I hated that she was moving so quickly. I knew she didn't have many people here that she knew. Well, only me and Ashahve and her family. The problem, though, was that I didn't want to get attached to her, like I did with Ashahve, only for her to pull away from me. When someone showed genuine interest in me, it was hard to not get attached. I yawned so hard, it made my eyes water. "Great, Elijah. Text me your address and I'll see you tomorrow afternoon. I'm gonna let you go. You sound so tired."

"I am. I didn't get a lot of sleep last night and I woke up early. I'll text you right now. See you tomorrow, Nyera."

"Okay. Bye."

I ended the call and sent the text, while thoughts flooded my mind. I didn't mind that she was wanting to spend time with me, I just hoped that her feelings about being around me didn't change when I revealed my battles with depression to her tomorrow. I didn't want to make the same mistake I'd made with Ashahve. My mind went back to her and how beautiful she looked in that tight dress and how it hugged her every curve. My mind went back even further, to the last time I'd seen her naked. Oh, how I wish I would have made love to her that night in Memphis.

She was so damn fine. Nyera was fine, too, but she wasn't Ashahve Glasper. Nyera was on the thinner side, but she was toned. She had a nice ass, too, but again, Ashahve was 'oh my Lord' fine. As I stared at the ceiling, I was wishing that time would repeat itself. While I often thought about Ashahve, tonight was torture. Being with Nyera and finding out that they were related wouldn't help matters. I only hoped that I wouldn't think of Ashahve too much while she was here. I rolled over to my side and hoped that sleep would soon summon me and put my mind out of its misery.

WHEN I WOKE UP, it was almost ten in the morning. I jumped from the bed, because I was almost sure Nyera would be arriving soon to cook. After handling my hygiene, including washing my hair, I oiled my beard and got dressed. I'd allowed my hair to grow out some and I regretted it. I hated having to maintain it. Next week, I'd be sure to make a trip to my barber.

I straightened up the house and made sure the kitchen was clean. My house usually stayed pretty clean because I cleaned up after myself daily. I couldn't stand clutter. After wiping down the counter-tops, I fixed a bagel with cream cheese and took my medication with some orange juice. I was still on the strong stuff, since my suicide attempt, a little over two months back. Every day had been a little easier to make it through, as time went on. I thought about Taylor occasionally, but not as often as I did right after my attempt.

After putting on some soft jazz, I got a text from Nyera saying she was on her way. Then, right after, I noticed that I'd also gotten a message from Ashahve. I was surprised, but happy. The message read: *I don't have a problem with you dating Nyera. I just pray that she never wants to bring you to my parents' house while Omari is there. That would be rather awkward. Plus, my mama knows I had a thing for an Elijah because of the flower incident.*

I'd forgotten all about those damn flowers I'd sent to her parents' house. Five huge arrangements were delivered there, scaring her mama half to death. Ashahve was so angry with me, at first. Geez! It would be difficult to date Nyera if she wanted to spend a lot of time there. That was her aunt and uncle's house and her only family here. I had a feeling that this would get interesting.

I responded to Ashahve. *I'll make sure that I won't attend if I know Omari will be there. Just text me and let me know and I'll make up an excuse why I can't go.*

After a minute or two, she responded. *Okay. Thanks.*

I ran my hand down my face and exhaled loudly. Nyera was a sweet woman and I wouldn't have a logical explanation for not seeing her again. As I let my thoughts wander aimlessly through my mind, the doorbell rang. I knew it had to be her, so I went to the front door to greet her. She stood there with two grocery bags in her hands, so I immediately took them from her and invited her inside. "Hey, Elijah."

"Hey. How are you?"

"I'm great. You have a beautiful home," she said, as she followed me to the kitchen.

"Thanks."

Once I sat the bags down, I grabbed her hand and kissed it. She blushed, then slid her hand away from mine. "So. What are you cooking?"

"I thought I would see how you liked my chicken spaghetti."

"Well, I like chicken spaghetti. So, tell me what I can do to help."

I watched her eyes widen slightly, like she wasn't used to a man wanting to do things for or with her. She walked closer to me, then asked, "Can I hug you?"

I didn't answer her verbally, just stretched out my arms, welcoming her into my embrace. When she hugged me, my entire body heated up. For some reason, that reminded me that I needed to talk to her about my issues with depression. She released my neck, then blushed again. I smiled at her, then got a couple of pots and a pan out. I noticed she had garlic toast as well. As I helped her get everything prepped and we small-talked, I said, "Nyera, I need to tell you something."

"Uh oh. What's up? Sounds serious."

I turned to face her, right there at the kitchen sink. My heart rate skyrocketed, and I could hear it beating in my ears. "I, uh... I have issues with depression."

"Okay. How serious is it?"

I took a deep breath. "It's serious. I'm on medication. I've attempted suicide twice."

Her eyes widened and she got quiet. She focused her gaze on something else. I continued to make the sweet tea, then put it in the fridge. I leaned against the door, once I closed it. "Nyera, I understand if that's too much for you to take on right now. You don't have to be afraid to say how you feel about that. If you want to ask questions, it's okay."

She nodded her head, then looked at me. "Let me think for a moment."

"No problem. I know it's a lot."

I started making the salad, somewhat in my feelings. Depression was a serious condition to have to deal with. It was scary when it was as serious as mine was. I understood her hesitation and her needing time to think. Telling her now was the right thing to do. Had I waited and gotten attached to her, things could get a little hairy.

"Elijah?"

"Yes?"

"When did you get diagnosed?"

My eyes went up, fishing for the correct answer. "About five years ago. It was after my ex-fiancée had left me for another man and I found out that, the whole time she was with me, she was planning her wedding to marry him instead."

Her eyebrows went up as her eyes widened for like the third time since she'd been here. "Oh, wow."

I nodded as I tossed the cherry tomatoes in the bowl with the sliced almonds and shredded carrots. She remained quiet for a while, as she put the noodles in a pan with sliced blocks of Velveeta cheese. "What happened when you found out?"

"I choked her and got in a fight with her husband. I got arrested and had to go to trial for attempted murder. The case was thrown out. I wasn't trying to kill her. I was mad as hell, though."

"I can imagine," she said softly.

She looked tense, and I wished there was something I could do to ease her tension. The fact that she was still here, after I told her all that, was shocking me. I was sure she would have bolted by now, especially after I mentioned attempted murder. I wrapped the salad bowl and slid it in the fridge to keep it cool. After turning the oven on and setting it to 350 degrees, I checked the chicken that was boiling on the stove. It looked to be done.

"When was the last time you attempted suicide?"

"A couple of months ago. My ex had resurfaced and was trying to talk to me. I refused. She was the reason I'd been diagnosed with depression. The hardships of trying to find a job and having to depend on my parents until I did was a lot to bear. A couple of weeks after she'd resurfaced, she pulled out in front of an eighteen-wheeler and was killed. I knew she did it intentionally. She suffered from bipolar disorder. I'd found that out from her mother a week prior to that. I felt so guilty about it. In my mind, I felt like she was reaching out to me for help and I turned her away."

I took a deep breath, trying not to relive how I felt. Talking about Taylor was difficult enough but having to talk about her death and the events afterward was pure torture. I got through it as quickly as possible. "Because of my guilt, I felt it was only right that I died, too. I overdosed on my medication."

"I'm so sorry."

I only nodded my head. "I'll be right back."

I walked out of the kitchen, because I needed to go do my exercises the counselor had taught me to do when I felt stressed, overwhelmed or down. The tension had set in my shoulders already. Going to my bedroom, I sat on the bed and took several deep breaths, holding the air inside for a few seconds before exhaling. That had calmed me down significantly, so I went back to the kitchen.

When I got in there, Nyera smiled at me. "You okay?"

"Yeah. I'm good."

I smiled back at her as I helped her shred the chicken. Hmm. She was accepting of my issues, it seemed. I didn't want to ask until later. My exercises would have been for nothing had I brought it up again so soon. It seemed like she understood that. Maybe today wouldn't be so bad after all.

Once she'd slid the spaghetti in the oven to bake, I set the timer, and we sat on the couch talking about random things until my doorbell rang. To say I had a moment of déjà vu was an understatement. It was the first time Ashahve had entered my mind since Nyera had been here. "Excuse me, Nyera."

I went to the door with a frown on my face. When I opened the door, I realized it was only UPS, dropping off a package from the sociological study of impoverished, Black single mothers I'd been involved in. It was the breakdown of the results. I'd requested it in written form, so I could use it as an example in my research methods class next semester. Thank God.

When I returned, Nyera was playing on her phone. "I'm sorry. It was UPS."

"Oh, it's no problem. I was just texting Ashahve to see if she wanted to go get mani-pedis one day this week."

I swallowed hard, because my mouth watered at the mention of Ashahve's name. Sitting next to her, we resumed our conversation about school, and how excited she was to be a professor at Lamar. She had a doctorate degree already and she was only twenty-six. That was extremely impressive. Most people didn't obtain their doctorate degree until they were at least twenty-eight. Brains ran in the family.

We continued to talk until the oven alerted us that it was time to check the spaghetti. Both of us went to the kitchen and I took the spaghetti out and she slid the garlic toast in. She, then, walked over to the stove where I'd sat the pan of spaghetti and stirred it. "It's perfect. We'll let it sit for a little bit, while the garlic toast is in the oven."

She smiled brightly and I smiled right back. Maybe, just maybe, Nyera would be the one for me.

A shahve

"So, how was dinner last night with Omari? He looked like he wanted to do damage to you in that dress."

"Mama!"

I'd just gotten home, and she had me all kinds of embarrassed. I guess since I'd never had a boyfriend that I felt as strongly for, we never talked about sex. The conversation was usually her trying to persuade me not to have sex at all but, if I did, to make sure I protected myself. "Oh, girl! You're twenty-three. I know you and Omari are having sex. I'd be a fool if I didn't. There is no way you spending nights at his place and not having sex. He too fine to turn down."

I dropped my head and shook it slowly. Omari was way too fine to turn down, and now that I knew he possessed gifts that had to come straight from God Himself, there was no way in hell I'd refuse to let him use those gifts on me. "Mama, he told me he loved me last night."

"What! Let me quit playing. I already knew that," she said, then laughed. "I can see it every time he looks at you. I can tell that you love him, too."

I smiled softly at her. "I do. He'll be here in an hour or so with Jordynn. I wanted to come home and get comfortable before he brought her."

"I'm happy for you, baby."

"Thanks, Mama."

I went to my room and laid across the bed, thinking about how well Omari had pleased my body last night. He had been holding back on me. I didn't realize it until the emotions took me over. He loved me tenderly, then roughly, passionately, then hard. He fucked me, made love to me, and fucked me again. I didn't know whether I was coming or going. Love wasn't a word that I threw out there without caution, but I knew that Omari had buried himself deep inside me... figuratively and literally.

After taking a shower and moisturizing, I decided to send a message to Dr. Coleman. I didn't want to respond around Omari. He wanted me to focus on him and I didn't mind doing that. We'd had an amazing night. I told Dr. Coleman that I didn't have a problem with him dating Nyera. I was actually glad he was seeing someone else. I also explained to him how awkward it would be if she brought him to my parents' house, though.

He understood and responded that if she ever wanted to go to a gathering, he would make up an excuse as to why he couldn't attend. I didn't respond to that, because if they ever got serious, that would be hard for him to keep doing without exposing our past. Nyera would never forgive either of us.

I heard Jordynn yell, "Na-Na!"

I smiled, then stood from my bed to meet them in the front room. When I got up there, Omari's eyes met mine and he made his way to me to kiss my lips. It was like we didn't just see each other a couple of hours ago. "Hi, Shavi!"

Jordynn hopped into my arms. "Hey, my lil sweet thang."

She smiled as I kissed her cheek, then set her on her feet. I looked back at Omari to find him still staring at me. He smiled, then said, "I don't have to be to work for another hour, but I wanted you to go somewhere with me before I went."

I glanced over at Mama and she tilted her head to the door with a smile on her face. After smiling back at her, I turned back to Omari. "Okay."

Going back to the room, I put my shoes on and headed out the door with him. We took the ten-minute drive to the cemetery on Pine Street. At that point, I knew what we were here for. Once he parked, he grabbed the flowers from the backseat, and we headed to her plot. "Baby, I was gonna open your door. You gon' have my mama mad at me for not being a gentleman."

I smiled softly at his attempt to make light of what we were doing here. "It's her birthday," he said.

My hand trembled in his. Although I didn't know his mother, I knew how much she'd meant to him. Omari glanced over at me and smiled. When we got to her gravesite, he looked over at me. "This doesn't bother me nearly as much as it did last year. Because of you, it's gotten even easier. I used to come here once a month and now, this is my first time coming here in three months. So, I wanna introduce her to the woman that has changed my whole life. You feel me, shawty?"

I gently caressed his cheek. "I feel you, baby."

He went to his knees, so I did as well. "Hey, Ma. I brought a visitor with me, this time. I know I never bring anybody other than Jordynn, but I finally found the one. I'm in love with her, Ma. Her name is Ashahve. I know you would have had a time trying to remember that, so we call her Shavi for short."

I gently shoved him as he laughed. He continued to talk as I sat there admiring him for the man he was. This was a different side. He wasn't as rude as he was before. However, I knew that side of him wasn't gone, it was only lying dormant. Before we left, I saw him get serious for a moment. He talked about how Jordynn was living with him full-time and how Piper had abandoned her. Then, he said, "I miss you, Ma. I wish you could see the man I'm evolving into. I love you."

A tear fell from his eye, but he quickly swiped it. That shit made them fall from my eyes. He stood, then helped me up. "Sorry, shawty," Omari said as he wiped the tears from my eyes. "Why you crying?"

"Seeing the tear drop from your eye and hearing the last of your words, made them fall."

He kissed my forehead. "Come on, shawty."

Before we could get back to my parents' house, my phone chimed with a text from Nyera. Omari looked over, as I responded to her about getting mani/pedis. "Nyera wants to go to the salon to get our nails and feet done."

I said that to ease his mind. I didn't want him to think it was Elijah. Shit, I was hoping it wasn't him either. He got attached quickly and I was hoping me communicating with him didn't come back to bite me in the ass. "Oh, okay. Shawty, you didn't have to tell me who texted you. I trust you. If it's something you think I should know, I trust you to tell me."

Damn. "Thank you, baby. You keep talking like that, you gon' be late to work."

"Normally, I would have taken yo' ass up on that, but I need to save my days for if my baby get sick and for the first day of school. That's aight, though. I'ma tear that pussy up as soon as you get to my place."

He glanced at me, then put his eyes back on the road. "You know, if you ever wanted to just stay with us, it wouldn't be a problem."

"Are you asking me to move in, Omari?"

I watched his face redden and a smile play on his lips. He

glanced over at me. "I guess I am. Can you see yourself living with me and baby girl?"

I stroked his cheek as he turned in my parents' driveway. "I can most definitely see me living with y'all, but let's wait a little while. Okay?"

"Aight, shawty. Just so you know, a nigga patient as hell when it comes to yo' ass."

I giggled, then leaned over and kissed his lips. "Thank you for taking me with you today. I know it was hard for you to show me your vulnerable side. By the way you speak about your mama, I can tell she was an amazing woman. I'll be by your place when I get off."

"That she was. What time you go in?"

"Not until four."

"Aight, baby. If you tired when you get off, you know I'll understand."

"Well, shit. One minute you want me to move in and the next you trying to get out of seeing me. You bipolar or what?"

"Man, get'cho ass outta here. You know I wanna see you. Especially so that pussy can sing for me like it did last night."

"Well, don't threaten me with a good time. Have a good day at work, daddy."

"Uh huh. Keep on an you gon' have to promote me from daddy to master. I don't wanna call in, but I will, to put this work on you."

"Well... call in. I'll call in, too. You know Mama don't mind watching Jordynn."

"You know I love yo' ass if I'm contemplating missing my money."

"But aren't I better than money?"

"Hell fucking yeah. But get out, for real, shawty."

"Okay, okay. I'm gone. See you when I get off."

I kissed his lips again and peeled myself from his seat. Omari Richard Watson was gonna be the death of me. My body responded to him in ways I'd never imagined. My damn underwear was drenched. After I got out, he peeled off. My shenanigans put him behind schedule. He liked to get to work ten minutes early and now he only had fifteen minutes to get there. It was every bit of a ten-minute drive from my parents' house.

When I walked in the house, Jordynn was riding her stationary horse that my mama had found at a garage sale, having the time of her life. Her hanging braids were bouncing as much as she was. "Shavi! You back!"

She hopped off her horse and ran to me. This little girl was so easy to love. I sat on the couch and she joined me, climbing right onto my lap. "Can we take a picture?"

"We sure can. How about we take a few?"

She nodded her head excitedly as I pulled my phone from my pocket. "You have to make cute poses. Then we'll send them to your daddy."

We ended up having a mini photoshoot, which we both thoroughly enjoyed. We did so many poses, Omari's phone would be receiving text messages for an hour. After I sent him a few, Mama said from the kitchen, "Jordynn, are you ready for your lunch?"

"Yes, ma'am. Can Shavi have lunch, too?"

"Do you wanna eat, Shavi?"

"Yes, ma'am."

Jordynn smiled at me, then kissed my cheek. "Are you going to marry Da-dy?"

My eyebrows lifted slightly. "I don't know. Maybe. Did he say he wanted to marry me?"

"No. But he was looking at rings on his phone that a lady was wearing in a wedding dress."

"Rings?"

"Yes. Come on, let's go eat."

Omari was thinking about marriage? He'd die if he knew Jordynn was spilling the beans. When we walked in the kitchen, Mama was staring at me wide-eyed. I shrugged my shoulders and sat at the table to eat my sandwich. As I sat there thinking, I couldn't help but wonder if Omari wanted Jordynn to tell me. He knew she was a little recorder and would play anything back at any given moment. Maybe he wanted her to gauge how I would feel about it. That was smart if that was the case. "Na-Na, I like the sandwich."

"Thank you, baby."

"Mommy, you like the sandwich, too?"

My eyes widened for the second or third time today. I glanced at my mama to see her watching. "Jordynn, you called me Mommy."

"Oh, silly me. I meant to say Shavi."

She was too grown for her age. But I didn't think that was a mistake. She was too calm about it. Omari and his lil daughter were trying to run game on me. I sent him a text. *Jordynn called me Mommy!*

She sat in her chair eating and swinging her legs happily. My phone chimed, alerting me of a text. Omari only sent laughing emojis. *I knew it!* They were plotting on me. "Shavi?"

"Yes, sweetheart?"

"Is my mommy ever gonna come back?"

"I don't know, baby girl."

"Well... can I call you Mommy sometimes?"

Her eyes were hopeful. I couldn't tell her no and I didn't know what else to say, so I only said, "We have to talk to your daddy about that. Okay?"

She smiled. "Okay. He's gonna say yes."

I scratched my head and shook it slowly. Omari and I had only been together for a couple of months. We'd known one another for almost four months. That was still too soon for her to wanna call me Mommy in my opinion, but there was no way I could tell her that. She seemed to be so content and I couldn't be responsible for making her sad. After Jordynn and I finished our lunches, we went to my room to take a nap.

❧ 6 ❧

O mari

"WHY YOU GOTTA BE SO GOT DAMN evil, Omari?"

"Naw! Evil is leaving your little girl, for a whole fucking month, without even a phone call to see how she's doing. That shit is heartless. You know how much she cried for you after the first week? How many times she cried herself to sleep wondering where the fuck her Mommy was at? So, naw, I ain't evil."

I ended the call. Piper had gotten served. I'd gone to a lawyer to file abandonment charges and get full custody of my baby. If someone would have told me, a year ago, that I would be going through this with Piper, I would have called them a liar. She always took care of Jordynn. My baby never looked neglected or nasty and her hair was always combed. So, when she dropped Jordynn off to me, that night, I was stunned.

We were already in July and the summer was almost over. Jordynn would be starting school in a couple of weeks and Ashahve and I would be starting in another month or so. It would be her last semester before she graduated with her bachelor's degree in sociology. Then, she would start graduate school the very next semester. So, I didn't have time to be dealing with Piper's bullshit, but for my baby girl to be happy, I'd take on the world.

When I got off work, I headed to the Glasper's house to pick up my baby. I also had some money for Mrs. Glasper. She always kept my baby free of charge and was teaching her things. She already knew her ABCs and her colors, but she'd taught her how to write her letters and numbers and how to spell her name.

She would be well ahead of her pre-k class, once school started. When I pulled in the driveway, Jordynn was in the backyard with Mrs. Glasper in the garden. She had on a straw hat that practically covered her face and she wore gloves that were as big as her arms. I chuckled as I got out of the car and snapped a picture of her. She was too cute.

When she saw me approaching, she yelled, "Da-dy! I got on Papa boots!"

I looked down to the oversized rubber boots she had on and laughed, then took another picture. She could barely walk in them. "Hey, princess. What are you doing?"

"Me and Na-Na are planting seeds!"

I picked her up, as the boots slipped off her feet, and kissed her cheek. "Hey, Omari. How was work?" Mrs. Glasper asked.

"It was good. This little lady didn't give you any trouble, did she?"

"Of course not. That's my angel."

"I have something for you. I know you always say I don't have to pay you, but please take this money. You do way more than just watch my baby. I can't let you do that for free."

She snatched the envelope from me as I laughed. I looked at my phone for the time, and it was nearly six. Ashahve was getting off at seven. "Well, you ready to go home, baby girl?"

"I wanna see Mommy."

I dropped my head. Piper was a fucking thorn in my flesh. It was probably wrong of me to think this way, but I often wished that Jordynn would forget about her. Before I could respond to her, she said, "Na-Na said she gets off in a little while."

My eyebrows had risen. Baby girl wasn't talking about Piper. She was talking about Ashahve. "Shavi?"

"Yes. I call her Mommy now."

"Oh, really?"

"Da-dy! Yes!"

I smiled at her and breathed a sigh of relief. The Lord knew I didn't have the patience to deal with Piper today. I could have strangled her just from the phone conversation. "Shavi is coming over to our house when she gets off."

"Okay!"

She started taking off her things as Mrs. Glasper laughed. Before we could leave, a car pulled in the driveway behind me. When the car door opened and she got out, I saw it was Nyera, Shavi's cousin that we'd met, at Floyd's, two months ago. She and Shavi had been hanging out a little. Once a week, they'd go to lunch and every other week, they'd go get their nails and feet done. "Hey, Auntie! Hey, Omari!"

"What's up, shawty."

"Era!"

"Hey, Jo Jo!"

Jordynn giggled at her nickname for her. They hugged and Nyera looked up at me. "I'm sorry, I'm blocking you in, but I promise I won't be but a minute."

She smiled then turned her attention to Mrs. Glasper. "Auntie, do you think I could use Grandma's old sewing machine? I wanna start making a sweater for my boyfriend. I hadn't made one in a while. So, I know, by the time I finish, it will probably be October."

They both laughed. "Sure. So, what's this boyfriend's name?"

"Elijah."

"Oh, wow! Ashahve used to talk to someone named Elijah, until he got a little weird on her."

"Really? I doubt it's this Elijah, though. He was her sociology professor."

Mrs. Glasper frowned slightly, then said, "Hmm. Okay. She went to Memphis with him for a conference a few months ago."

Fuck. I could tell that her wheels were turning. "Yes, he told me about that."

"Well, come on inside."

Looks like Ashahve was gon' be explaining to her mama why she was messing around with her professor, sooner rather than later.

༺✿༻

"Yo, Rich!"

I looked up from the tire I was mounting, to see one of my co-workers trying to get my attention. "What's up?"

"Can you say about how much longer on the Maxima? The customer's debating on whether they are going to wait or not."

"About fifteen minutes. I'm mounting the last tire now."

"Okay. Thanks."

I'd just gotten here, and it had been a rough day already. Last night was a long one. After talking to Ashahve about Nyera and her mother's discussion about Elijah Coleman, Jordynn had woken up screaming, during one of our love-making sessions. I'd planned to go to sleep right after I'd put that kitty to sleep, but Jordynn had had a nightmare and was scared to go to sleep. She didn't eventually fall asleep until four this morning. I had to be to work at eight and it was only noon.

Ashahve had nearly shit on herself when I told her that it looked like her mother was putting two and two together. She was gonna figure out, before long, that her Elijah and Nyera's Elijah were the same person. I really didn't see what she saw in that nigga, but whatever. Usually you could figure out a woman's specific type of man by looking at who she dated, but the two of us were like night and day.

I was an outspoken, bold nigga that didn't give a fuck about hurting nobody's feelings. Sensitivity was something I lacked, and my personality was hood as fuck. That professor, though, seemed soft as hell. He was the intellectual type. We had about the same build, but that was it. Maybe she just liked muscular types. That was about the only thing we had in common.

Once the car was ready, I walked inside with the keys and the work order, then called out, "Laken Poullard?"

When shawty stood, I recognized her from Lamar. I had a class with her, last semester. She smiled and said, "What's up? I didn't know you worked here."

"Yeah. What's up, shawty? How's your summer going?"

"It's aight. I'm in summer school. The summer session will be over in two weeks."

"Oh, okay. That's what's up. Well, good to see you."

Before I could walk away, she called out, "Omari?"

"Yeah?"

"You umm... wanna hang out some time?"

"I'm sorry, shawty, but I got a girl."

"Oh. My bad."

"It's cool. Be easy, lil mama."

I walked away and noticed she'd watched me until I was out of sight. She was bad and had a nice shape, she was just a lil too bougie for my tastes. I'd seen her shoot niggas down, left and right and look down her nose at people. She thought she wanted to hang with me. Shiiid, I'd hurt her lil bougie feelings. Ashahve was all the woman I needed. With as freaky as her ass was, she was all the woman I could handle. I didn't see how niggas juggled so many women.

I gave Shavi one hundred percent, with everything I did for her. There wasn't room or energy to be trying to cater to nobody else. And, if I took five percent from Shavi to give to somebody else, she would know something was up immediately. She knew I didn't half-step in none of the shit I did. It was all or nothing. We'd gotten to know one another so well we could finish each other's sentences. So, there was no way I would even get cocky enough to think I could pull the wool over her eyes.

Before putting my gloves back on, I texted Ashahve just to tell her I loved her. I tried to do that at least once during my shift so she would know I was thinking about her. She was always thinking about me and I appreciated her for that. She came with me to the cemetery, again, last month and had brought a poetry book called When Night Comes by this chick named Jess Words, so I could read it while we sat there. Shawty that wrote that book was fire, for real. My mama would have loved that shit.

Just as I was putting my gloves back on, so I could get the day over with, Shavi texted back. *I love you, too. Can't wait to see you.* I smiled at it, then got back to work.

The rest of the day flew by, and Shavi had texted me to say that she and Jordynn were already at the apartment. I was glad, because there was nothing that I wanted more than a shower. I'd sweat my ass off. We were so busy today, it was unreal. What was crazy, though, was that when we closed, I saw Laken riding by, like she was just that infatuated with a nigga. I could see her eyes darting from one side of the parking lot to the other, like she was looking for me.

I'd never seen Ashahve's crazy side and I had no desire to see that shit come out. Every woman had a crazy side, when they felt threatened. Look at how the fuck Piper was acting. Our court date was coming up soon, so I was hoping that she let that crazy-ass side come out in court. My baby girl had been living with me for almost three months and I'd gotten her enrolled in school already. It would hurt like hell if the judge took my baby from me. I'd gotten used to seeing her beautiful smile every day and holding her in my arms at night until she went to sleep. Ashahve had gotten attached to her as well. That attachment only grew stronger when Jordynn started calling her Mommy, last week.

After getting in my car, I cranked up that Dedication track by

Nipsey Hussle and rode out. It was a shame what happened to that brother. Before I could even get a mile down the road, my phone was ringing. It was Ashahve. "Hey, baby. I just left work. I should be there in ten minutes."

"Omari... umm..."

"What's up, shawty? Spit that shit out."

"Piper is here, demanding that I let her see Jordynn."

"Hell naw! Tell her ass... better yet, put me on speaker."

"Okay. You're on."

"Piper, have yo' ass there when I get there. How you gon' demand to see somebody you didn't have the decency to see about for a whole fucking month? You go inside my apartment and I'm gon' call the cops on yo' ass."

"As much as you may hate me, Rich, I'm still Jordynn's mother. I have a right to see my daughter!"

"Not if I ain't there, you don't. Wait your ass outside! You not gon' see my baby without my supervision. I don't trust yo' ass. Shavi, if she try to get her ass in my apartment before I get there, call the police. I should be there in five minutes, baby."

"Okay, Omari."

"I'm sorry you in the middle of the bullshit, baby."

"It's okay. I got'chu."

That made me smile. "Aight, girl. Love you."

I ended the call and changed the music, to mellow out. If I was listening to this rap shit, I was liable to fuck Piper up. I changed it to some shit Ashahve had downloaded to my phone by Terrace Martin. By the time I got home, I was calm as hell. Piper was sitting her ass on my porch, on a chair that Ashahve had to have given her. I got out the car slowly, trying to dwell on the smooth sounds that had come from my radio.

When I approached, she stood from her seat. I couldn't stop the frown that made its way to my face. *Calm down, Rich.* Only people from school and people I felt something for actually called me Omari. Everyone else called me Rich. When Piper and I first broke up, I wouldn't respond to her when she called me Omari. She was fucking some other nigga, but blamed that shit on me, saying I'd checked out on her emotionally.

I *had* checked out on her, but my mama, my rock, had died. She should've been there for me during that time instead of complaining about me not being there for her. Even if she couldn't be there for me, she should have just broken up with me instead of fucking around. Through all that, though, Jordynn was my only constant. She was the only female that loved me unconditionally and could make my heart turn soft like Jell-o.

"Look, Rich. I'm sorry. I fucked up. You don't have to keep reminding me. But I miss Tutu. That's my baby and I was wrong for using her to try to prove a pointless statement. You have who you want in your life, and she treats Tutu like a princess. Just seeing you so happy with someone else is devastating to me. I still love you, and you know that. I fucked that up, too. Just don't keep Tutu from me."

She said all that before I could go off on her ass. Smart. The frown left my face and I opened the door and let her walk in. She smiled at me as the tears fell down her cheeks. When she walked in, Jordynn started screaming and ran to her. Walking over to Ashahve near the kitchen, I kissed her lips. "Thank you, baby."

"You don't have to thank me. I told you I got'chu."

"Hi, Da-dy! Look! Mommy came to see me!"

I kissed my princess. "I see, baby."

She was so excited, and it was at that moment that I regretted keeping her from her mama this past month. While I thought I was protecting her from hurt, I was the one causing it. I watched her run back to her mama and sit on the couch, then gave my attention back to Ashahve. I slowly pushed her to the back, out of sight. Staring into her eyes, I could see her unraveling in my presence. I licked my lips and pulled her close to me. "Omari..."

"What's up, Ashahve?"

"Stop," she said breathlessly.

"Stop what, Ashahve?"

"First of all, you know what it does to me to hear you say my name like that. Secondly, you looking at me like I'm a snack."

"Shawty, you ain't a snack. You a seafood buffet."

She fell out laughing, dropping her head back. I took the opportunity to kiss her neck and nibble at the flesh right beneath her earlobe. Her sharp intake of air caused her laughing to cease. Whispering in her ear, I said, "What's wrong, shawty? You want daddy inside yo' pussy, huh?"

Her hand went to the back of my head, as I listened to Jordynn scream with laughter. She lifted her head and kissed my lips, then slipped her hand to my crotch and squeezed my dick. "You stink so good, Omari. All man and that shit is turning me on. I ain't never had a man's funk turn me on. Get away from me."

I kissed her lips again, gently sucking her bottom one, then backed away from her. I couldn't wait to dig up in her shit. It had been a few days since I'd had a taste and my damn mouth was watering, anticipating the feel of her juices on my lips. As *soon* as Jordynn went to sleep tonight, that pussy was mine.

7

E lijah

THIS THING with Nyera was trying to get serious, but I wasn't ready. I thought I was, but after seeing Ashahve, a couple of days last week, I knew it was too soon. We'd gone to Bath and Body Works, once, while she was at work, and another time we'd gone to her parents' house. Nyera was sweet and I really liked her, but I still loved Ashahve. When the semester was over, I thought I would have all summer to get her out of my system. That was impossible, since I was seeing her almost once a week now.

I was going to eventually have to tell Nyera about me and Ashahve's past. Maybe not every detail of it, but just that we'd kissed and shared a moment of passion. But that could also lead to problems. I'd been sitting on my enclosed patio all morning, trying to think of a way to handle the situation. Since Nyera and I hadn't had sex, I knew I needed to tell her before or if we ever got to that. Sex tended to complicate things, especially for me.

I really got attached to Ashahve, after our time in South Padre Island. I hadn't been able to shake her since. Although I'd been able to keep my distance, physically, she was still in my thoughts... my dreams. I supposed since I'd fantasized about her, for so long, before we actually went to that level, it made me fall for her even quicker. Nyera had a doctor's appointment this morning and had to meet with the nursing department chair at Lamar.

Looking at my phone, I couldn't help but scan through pictures of Ashahve. I'd put them in a vault app, just so I could look at how sexy she was. She seemed so happy, but I had to let her know how much she still meant to me. Grabbing my phone, I looked at the time to see it was almost noon. I sent a text. *Hello. I just wanted to see how you were doing. Have a good day.*

Holding the phone in my hand, I continued to scan pictures and came across one that made my heart beat rapidly. She was in a bikini, in South Padre Island. My mind recalled all the freaky things we did out there and how I quickly fell in love with her. She was everything I wanted in a future wife; passionate, driven, intelligent and beautiful, inside and out. Shavi was fine as hell and could bring the hardest man to his knees, simply from her touch.

She texted back. *Hey! I'm great! How are you? How are things with you and Nyera?*

My heart quickened even more so. She didn't close off the conversation and that made my heart feel amazing. I responded, *I'm great. Things are progressing between us, but I'm a little hesitant.*

If she asked why, then I'd gladly tell her. I needed a damned drink. As I went inside and poured a glass of wine, she messaged back. *I think I know where this is going, but I'm gonna ask anyway. Why?*

I smirked. She was only exhibiting the qualities I loved about her. She cared too much to not ask why. Before grabbing my glass from the countertop, I responded. *I still love you. Being with her, at your parents' house, and seeing you so often isn't helping me get over you. I love you, Shavi.*

I grabbed my glass and headed back to my seat outside. Sitting it down on the small round table, I laid back in the lounger, waiting to see if she would respond. After taking a couple of sips of my wine, I started to relax a bit. My phone chimed and I opened it to see her response.

Elijah, I know this isn't easy for you. It's not completely easy for me either. It's actually somewhat uncomfortable. However, I'm in love with Omari. We love each other. I know that wasn't what you wanted to hear, but I want you to move on. I want you to be happy. Nyera makes you happy. I could see that, last week, when I saw y'all. Consider progressing with her. Maybe she can make you forget about lil ol' me. I do care about you, Elijah, but Omari has my heart. He's who I want.

I felt gut checked for a minute. Once I settled my emotions, I responded. *You're not easy to get over. I'm glad you've found love and I'm glad you're happy. I'm trying to move on and hopefully, I can successfully. Again, I love you and I wish you the best.*

I gulped the rest of my wine. The way I was feeling was disturbing me. I knew she would turn me down, but to know that she was in love with him bothered me way more than it should have. What was it about him that she didn't have with me? When I got up to pour another glass of wine, the doorbell rang, signaling Nyera's arrival.

I took a few deep breaths, trying to calm down, then sat my glass in the sink. When I opened the door, she was standing there with a smile on her face. "Hey."

"Hey, sweetheart. Come on in."

She walked inside in her tight jeans and I licked my lips as I looked her body over. After closing the door, I turned to her and kissed her cheek. She blushed and shied away from me. We'd never even tongue kissed or kissed longer than a couple of seconds. Her plump lips were beckoning me to taste them all the time... to suck on that bottom one. I didn't want to push her away by moving too fast, but we'd been talking for over two months now.

I wanted to grab her by her natural coils and make passionate love to her, but if she wouldn't even kiss my lips longer than a few seconds, she'd break up with me, for sure, if I tried to make love to her. I grabbed her hand and led her further inside to sit on the couch. "So, how was your appointment and your meeting?"

"The doctor's appointment went well. He seems really nice. The meeting was a little stressful, but I can make the most out of a stressful situation. She was telling me all the meetings I'd have to attend, and how me and the other A&P professor should get close enough to be on a first name basis."

Hmm. Maybe the nursing program was stricter, but I didn't have to interact with any of the other sociology professors if I didn't want to. "Well, I believe you will handle it well. You have an amazing personality. Was the other A&P professor there?"

"Yes, he was there."

My interest piqued. So, it was a man. "Does it seem like it will run smoothly?"

"I hope so. That was my first time meeting him. He wasn't that talkative during the meeting."

"Oh."

I grabbed her hand and rubbed it between mine, trying to ignite a spark of some kind. Looking at Ashahve's photos earlier had me horny and I was on the verge of feeling deprived. She was the last person I had sex with, and that was over three months ago. I knew I was wasting my time and that Nyera wouldn't have sex with me, but maybe I could see some progress in that direction if I kept at it.

I scooted closer to her and kissed her hand, then her cheek. She stiffened some like she was nervous. Sliding my finger down her arm, I said, "Nyera, why do you seem nervous? We've been together for a couple of months. Shouldn't you be comfortable around me by now?"

She dropped her head for a moment. I decided to back off. Scooting back to my original spot on the couch, I let go of her hand. "I'm sorry. I'm not trying to rush you. Take your time, okay?"

She nodded, then smiled. "So, what are we doing today?"

"Whatever you want."

It didn't matter what we did. I was irritated already. My girl-friend was acting like she was afraid of me. I didn't know what her issue with me was, but I would let her tell me in her own time. My hand was gonna become reacquainted with my dick, though. I'd been trying to refrain from doing that, but I'd been so turned on, I was gonna get blue balls. "Can we go to Colorado Canyon?"

"Miniature golf?"

"Yeah. You don't think it will be fun?"

"I don't know. I've never played before. We can go. Let's go to lunch."

I grabbed her hand and helped her from the sofa so we could head out. Getting my mind off sex was my main agenda and that wouldn't happen as long as we were sitting in my house. When we got outside, my phone chimed with a message. I was pretty sure that it was from Ashahve. After opening Nyera's door for her to get in my car, I checked it. *I wish you the best, too, Elijah.*

I could hear her voice saying my name and that alone was turning me on. Naturally, that voice I heard was how she sounded the last time I made love to her. The way my name rolled off her tongue while she was moaning and screaming in ecstasy was too much to take. When I opened the door, I started the car. "I'll be right back, Nyera. I forgot to take my medicine."

I was lying to her, but I surely couldn't tell her that I needed to jack off. "Okay," she said nervously.

Whatever was up with her was making me wonder if she was the woman for me. We seemed to be so different, now. After walking in the house, I made a bee line to the restroom. Opening my phone, I immediately went to the sexy pictures of Ashahve. My dick was so hard, it was ridiculous. I knew I had to hurry, though, so I squirted some lotion in my hand and stroked my dick until I released what had to be ounces of cum, in the toilet.

As I flushed, I heard an engine start. Being that the bathroom was in the front of the house, I looked out the window to see if someone was in my driveway. The engine sounded super close. As I peered out, I saw Nyera backing out. *What the fuck?* I grabbed my phone from the countertop and called her. "Hello?"

"You're just gonna leave without telling me anything?"

"I... ummm... I'm sorry. It's just that, ever since you told me about your past, I've been extremely nervous around you. I can't continue a relationship with you that way."

"Nyera, that was over a month ago. You just realized that you had a problem with my past?"

"I'm sorry, Elijah."

"Okay. Whatever."

I ended the call and punched the wall. Here I was trying to be honest, from jump, and that shit bit me in the ass. Ashahve understood me. She was the one I should've been totally honest with in the beginning. How could Nyera do this to me? I was glad I hadn't fallen for her. I washed my hands and went outside to kill my engine.

My hand was hurting, so I'd probably broken my damn fingers. She could have been upfront with me about it, but I guess if I made her nervous, she probably thought I wouldn't respond to it well. When I got back inside, I put some ice in a bowl and put my hand in it. With the other hand, I texted Ashahve. *Nyera just broke up with me.*

She responded immediately. *What? Why?*

She said my past made her nervous. I told her everything a month ago. All the things I should've told you in the beginning. We were supposed to be going out, but I came back inside the house to use the restroom and she left without a word. When I called her, asking why she left, she told me that she couldn't continue a relationship with me, because I made her nervous.

I slid my phone in my pocket and carried the bowl of ice to the end table next to my recliner. Life was something else. Ashahve was angry because I hid my past from her and Nyera was nervous because I revealed my past to her. I couldn't win for losing. As I pulled my phone from my pocket, Ashahve texted back. *I'm so sorry, Elijah. Can I call you in a little bit?*

Hmm. That was interesting. Why did she want to call me? Whatever the reason, I'd be elated to speak with her and hear her voice. *Sure.*

I went to the kitchen and got a towel to wrap my hand, then took three Tylenol. Sitting back in my chair, I sank my hand in the ice as I cringed. It was swollen as hell, but I was praying nothing was broken. If the swelling didn't go down by morning, I'd have to go to the ER. As I laid back in the chair, my phone began ringing. "Hello?"

"Hi, Elijah. How are you?"

"I could be better."

"Look, don't tell Nyera I told you this, but she was once in an abusive relationship. Most likely, that's why your past is so hard for her to handle. She has an extremely difficult time talking about it. Her mama told my mama about the toxic relationship, and then we saw it online. He got charged with attempted murder. So, don't be so hard on her. You're the first guy she's tried to date since then."

Damn. I never took that into consideration. Never thinking that she had been through something as well. "Wow. How long ago did that happen?"

"It's been a little over four years, I think. I'd just graduated from high school."

"Wow. I'll give her time, then. But I also need to prepare for the fact that she may not wanna be with me. Luckily, I'm not attached to her."

Ashahve was completely quiet. She was probably thinking about how attached I was to her. "Well... umm... I have to go. I'm at work. I just wanted to tell you that."

"Thanks, Shavi."

"You're welcome."

She ended the call and I sat back in my recliner, trying to think of how I could get her to see me.

8

A shahve

"I REALLY TRIED, Shavi, but whenever I'm with him, I think I about all the bullshit I went through with Greg. I cannot go through that again. Greg started off being great, just like Elijah, then it was like a damned switch went off in his brain. The first time he hit me, that shit caught me by surprise. Then, I kept telling myself that it was my fault and that things would get better."

She shook her head slowly, as if she was sifting through those memories in her mind. "Dr. Coleman wouldn't hurt a fly, Nyera. He's really sweet and caring. We had conversations all the time, after class, about life from a sociological perspective."

"I don't doubt that he's sweet, but you're acting like you've been in a relationship with him. I'm just not willing to hang around and find out. Could I be missing out on the best thing to ever happen to me? Yeah, but being with him is a chance I'm not willing to take. I'm so happy I hadn't had sex with him."

This conversation was hard as hell. If she would have had sex with him, she would be willing to take that chance. His sex had me hanging around a lot longer than I should have, and I had options. However, I needed to change the subject before I started giving shit away. It was bad enough my mama was questioning me about him and our trip to Memphis. Hell, it was practically a good thing that they weren't going to work out.

Hopefully, he wouldn't start calling me again. I had to call to explain to him about Nyera's thought process, so he wouldn't give up, but she seemed pretty dead set on not being involved with him. Nyera had always been strong-minded, so when word got around about her and Greg, everyone was in shock. "Well, I'm not here to convince you to give him a chance. I'm here to applaud you for doing what was best for you."

"Thanks, cuz."

She leaned over and hugged me as my phone chimed. It was probably Omari, because I was supposed to meet him at his house when he got off. It was already seven. Looking at it to confirm it was him, my eyebrows lifted when I saw a message from an unknown number. I frowned slightly. Before I opened it, Nyera asked, "You okay?"

"I'm just tryna figure out who this is. The number isn't saved in my phone. They sent a picture."

I opened the message to see Omari with some chick at his job. They were standing there talking and holding hands. My ears got hot as hell. Omari wouldn't make a fool of me. He just wouldn't. But why in the fuck was he holding hands with this woman? "Shavi?" Nyera said, causing me to pull my eyes away from the picture. She rubbed my back, "Talk to him. Everything ain't what it seems."

"Says the woman that won't give Dr. Coleman a chance, based on what she's been through. Like you, I can't go through heartbreak like this again. My last boyfriend was a whole-ass fuck-boy. He was cheating on me almost the entire time. I can't go through that shit again, either."

"Whoever sent that to you tryna start some shit, Shavi. Ask who they are."

I looked back at my phone and could feel the lump forming in my throat as I stared at the picture. What made me angry was that I'd allowed myself to fall in love with him. He said he loved me. I'd gotten attached to a little girl that I would have to let go. It didn't matter who sent the picture or how they got my number. What mattered to me was knowing why he was holding this woman's hand. I forwarded the picture to him.

"You need to go talk to him. Jordynn is with your mama, right?"

"Yeah. I came straight here from work. When you called, I was just clocking out. I'm not going over there to talk to him, though. I can't."

Before she could respond, my phone rang. Omari.

"Yeah?"

"It's not what it looks like."

"Then, tell me, Omari. What exactly is it?"

"She was a customer and had grabbed my hand to thank me for fixing her tire."

"Really? How often does that usually happen? You looked extremely comfortable holding her hand."

"Shawty, you know me. I wouldn't do that shit to you."

"Did you see your facial expression on the picture, Omari? That's how you look at me! I don't have time for the bullshit! You wanna come at me straight, nigga?"

"First, you gon' lower your got damn voice. Secondly, the day I became your man, I was no longer a nigga. Get that in your mind right now and let that shit marinate. Thirdly, I ain't no fucking liar. If I said it was nothing, then you should believe that shit because I ain't gave you a reason not to."

I remained quiet, attitude on full 'cuss his ass out' mode, as he continued. "Now... she grabbed my hand to thank me for fixing her tire without charging her. I smiled and accepted her gratitude. She asked to take me to lunch. I slid my hand from hers and told her I had a woman. I ain't tryna fuck this up wit'chu, Ashahve."

"Whatever. It looks extremely suspect."

"Where are you? You need to be here so we can talk. I hate doing shit like this by phone."

"Well, I hate getting incriminating pictures of my *nigga* holding hands with another woman. But ain't shit I can do about that, is there?"

"See, you on that fuck-shit. Bring yo' ass over here, Ashahve, and quit acting like one of those ratchet-ass females. You know I'm a good man. I shouldn't have to prove shit that done already been proven."

He ended the call. I wanted to go off on his ass, for real. Let a picture had been sent to him of me and another nigga. He would have clowned me big time. I couldn't call him a nigga, but he could talk to me however he wanted to? I think not. Nyera was looking at me with a sympathetic expression on her face. "I have to go. I'll call you tomorrow. I'm off."

"Okay. Maybe we can go to lunch."

I stood from her couch and headed to the door. Omari's stubborn ass was probably gonna stay at my parents' house until I got there. Then my mama would be calling me to see where I was. I hated when they got involved in my business. When my ex and I broke up, Mama damn near knew more than I did about what went down. It irritated the hell out of me.

When I turned in the driveway, Omari was sitting on the back of his car. *Shit.* I wasn't ready for this argument. Mama probably knew what was going on, since he was sitting outside without Jordynn. I parked beside him and as soon as I emerged from my car, he hopped off his car. "I'm not trying to argue with you, Omari."

"Good, 'cause I ain't tryna argue wit'chu either."

I stared at him as he stared right into my eyes. Rolling my eyes, I was attempting to go inside, but he pulled me to him. "Look... if you don't believe me, then maybe we shouldn't be together. I need a woman that's gon' be down for her *nigga*. Obviously, whoever took the picture and sent that shit to you is somebody that want me to themselves. So, if you doubting me, maybe it's best we end this now, so we won't have this headache down the road. Just like you ain't got time for the bullshit, I ain't got time for it either."

"Well, I guess this saved us a lot of heartache then, huh?"

He nodded, then walked away from me and went inside the house. I followed behind him, not really wanting him to go, but not wanting to be made a fool of either. "Thank you, Mrs. Glasper for watching Jordynn. I'm off tomorrow and the weekend. I'll be enrolling her in a daycare."

He reached in his pocket and I could see him trembling. My mama was standing there with her mouth wide open. Omari put a wad of cash in her hand, then grabbed Jordynn and all of her things. "Shavi, you coming to our house?"

I could feel the tears making their way to my eyes. "No, baby. I love you."

"I love you, too," she said sadly.

Omari looked at me, one last time, and walked out the door. My heart was hurting. My mama was still standing there quietly, so I took the opportunity to go to my room and lock myself inside. I was scared of being hurt again by love. Every boyfriend from the time I was sixteen until now, had cheated on me. Why would he be any different? Why did I expect anything different? What was it about me that attracted cheaters?

Before long, I was bawling my eyes out. Although I was hoping I was wrong about him, it was too late. Omari was done with me, and he wasn't the type to beg for anything or anyone. He'd said that he wasn't built for the chase. So, if I was wrong, I'd just lost my good thing.

My forever.

My love.

My nigga.

As I laid in the bed, in the fetal position, there was a knock on my door. I knew it was my mama, but I just didn't feel like getting up to unlock the door. "I'm here if you wanna talk."

She sounded so upset. I knew it had everything to do with her not being able to see Jordynn anymore. I loved that little girl so much, maybe even more than I loved Omari. Knowing that I wouldn't see her anymore only made me cry harder. My phone chiming broke me from my pity party. It was a text from Omari. *Since I'm off tomorrow, I'll bring your things after I get shawty in daycare.*

I wiped my face. I messed up. He had to know that I was angry and that once I had time to think about it, I'd want to talk things out. *Can we talk tomorrow when you come? I'm off, too.*

I sat there for at least five minutes, waiting for his response. It seemed he wasn't going to give me one, so I walked to my personal bathroom within my bedroom and started the shower. As I was getting my bed clothes to bring in the bathroom, I heard my phone chime. I practically dove across my bed to snatch it from the nightstand. The moment I opened the message, I regretted it.

I wanted to talk today, shawty. That ship sailed when I walked out the door. I get that you were angry at what you saw, but a picture freezes a moment in time. So, while it looked like I was holding her hand forever, it only lasted a few seconds. Had we talked about this like adults, the shit wouldn't have gotten this far. Again, I'll bring your things tomorrow and I forgot a few of Jordynn's things as well.

I fucked up. Plugging the charger back to my phone, I sat it on the nightstand and drug myself to the shower. Tomorrow, I'd have to make sure I left early, so I didn't have to see him.

෧෨

WHEN I WOKE UP, it was nearly ten in the morning. I didn't finally fall asleep until three. My mind had been filled with possible strategies for getting Omari to take me back. Although, if he was as stubborn as I thought he was, there would be nothing I could do to persuade him. I got up and got dressed to head to Nyera's place.

After unlocking my door and walking down the hallway, I noticed Mama holding Jordynn as Omari walked inside. I literally wanted to go back in my room and hide until he left, but Jordynn had already seen me. "Shavi!"

She hopped out of my mama's arms and ran to me. "Hey, sweet cakes."

"Shavi, what's wrong?"

"Nothing. I'm okay. How are you?"

"You're crying. You missed me?"

"Yeah. That's exactly what it is. I missed you so much."

I hugged her tightly as Omari stared at me. "You shoulda came to our house. Me and Da-dy watched a mooovie. He painted my naaaii-ils. Rubbed my leeeegs."

"Sounds like y'all had fun," I said as I sat her on her feet.

"We did! You have to come next time."

I nodded as my mama said, "Jordynn, why don't we go in your room and see what you forgot."

"Okay!"

I stared at Omari and he stared right back. The lack of emotion in his eyes was tearing me apart and I couldn't take it. I walked past him to the door, halfway expecting him to grab my arm or try to stop me, but he didn't. That only further destroyed me inside. When I got to my car, I couldn't help but sit there and cry. I loved him, but I was stupid when I let him walk out of here last night.

As I started my engine, Omari and Jordynn were walking out with the rest of her clothes and two dolls. Jordynn smiled brightly as I started to cry harder. It felt like my heart was being ripped out of my chest. She noticed I was crying, and a frown made its way to her little face. I hurriedly wiped my tears as Omari watched me, then put the car in gear.

While I backed out, I could see Jordynn crying and Omari

wiping her tears. The look he gave me afterwards, let me know that there wasn't a chance in hell for me to be in his life again. My actions, or the lack thereof, had hurt the one person that meant the world to him. If I'd hurt Jordynn, I knew my position in his life had now been eliminated.

9

O mari

"Don't cry, baby girl."

"But Shavi was crying. Why she crying?"

"Let's not worry about that, okay? We're about to go see your new school. You ready?"

"Okaaay."

I hated to see Ashahve cry, but it was her own fault. She knew I would never hurt her. I'd told her and I thought my actions proved that, but maybe not. I couldn't concern myself with her insecurities and trust issues, especially being that I'd been good to her. I was a damned good man, and ain't nobody was gonna make me feel like less. I hated to take Jordynn away from Mrs. Glasper, too. To see her cry after we'd walked out the door did something to me. I had her phone number, so maybe I'd call her to come meet us for lunch or dinner sometimes.

When we got to the daycare, Jordynn seemed to be okay. I was far from it, though. I loved Ashahve, and this shit hurt. On top of the hurt was anger. She could have handled this situation a lot better than what she did. I was disappointed in her actions, and that was why the shit hurt. I thought she was better than that. Once we were inside, I talked to the receptionist and filled out paperwork as one of the teachers showed Jordynn around.

As I filled out the paperwork, my phone began ringing. Although I probably wouldn't answer her right now, I was hoping it was Ashahve. I looked at the screen to see it was Piper. "Hello?"

"Hey, Omari. Are you off today?"

"Yeah."

"You think it would be possible for me to see Tutu, today?"

"Yeah. Let me hit you back in a lil bit."

"You okay?"

"Yeah."

I ended the call. My mood was fucked, and I couldn't hide the shit. Maybe I should just call Ashahve so we could squash this and move on with our relationship. I loved her too much to just let what we had die over a misunderstanding. Then, at the same time, she wasn't calling me to try to work things out. My mind was all over the place, trying to decide what to do. Hopefully I filled the paperwork out right. All I could think about was Ashahve.

Once we left the daycare, I called Piper back and we agreed to meet at Chick-fil-a, so she could see Jordynn. Over the past week, she'd been showing that she was really sorry about abandoning our baby. Jordynn had been wanting to go to her house, but I kept making up excuses why she couldn't. Depending on how things went today, I'd probably let her go. When we got to Chick-fil-a, Jordynn's eyes lit up. "Yay! Can I play, Da-dy?"

"After you eat."

As I got her out of her car seat, I saw Piper drive up. She had a huge smile on her face and as soon as she parked, she jumped out of her car and ran to Jordynn. "Tutu!"

"Mommy!"

They were so excited to see each other. I watched her swing Jordynn around, then put her down. Piper looked up at me, toning her smile down some. "Hey, Rich. Thanks for meeting me."

I gave her a head nod, then walked inside and ordered Jordynn some chicken nuggets. "You want something, Piper?"

Her eyebrows rose slightly. "Can you get me some nuggets, too?"

"Aight."

I ordered her nuggets and a chicken sandwich for me. While she and Jordynn talked up a storm, I thought about things with Ashahve. Maybe I should just move on. When they called my number, I went to the front and got our food, then brought it back to the table. I could see Piper watching me, but I refused to acknowledge her. She was the last person I wanted to talk to about all my personal issues with Ashahve.

After spreading mayo on my sandwich, I began eating, tuning Piper's ass out. She was trying to talk to me, but I didn't wanna talk to anybody but Ashahve. *Why in the fuck was I torturing myself?* I grabbed my phone to just call her, but then my alter ego said, *She ain't worried about your ass. That's why she hadn't called you.*

It was like the angel and the devil were sitting on my shoulders. Omari was the angel and Rich was the devil. Rich was winning. I sat the phone on the table, and it started ringing right after. Hoping it was Ashahve, I was disappointed to see Mali's number, this chick I used to screw before Ashahve and I hooked up. "Yeah?"

"Hey, Rich. How are you?"

"I'm good. What's up?"

"Well, I know I had a hard time handling you the last time we messed around, but I wanted to see if you wanted to hook up?"

"Let me think on that, shawty. I'll hit'chu later."

"Okay."

Maaaan, I didn't wanna fuck Mali, but if that was gon' take my mind off Ashahve, I'd do it with the quickness. This level of hurt was foreign to me. Although Piper had fucked around on me, I realized that what I felt for her, back then, was nothing in comparison to how I feel for Ashahve. She had my heart on lock. But my stubbornness and my pride were keeping me from calling her. *Omari, quit tripping. It ain't like she cheated on you.* That was the angel. I was the one that looked to be in a compromising situation. Shavi was angry. She couldn't hear what I was trying to say because she was angry by what she thought she'd seen.

"Da-dy!"

I turned to Jordynn with a slight frown on my face, because she'd yelled. She giggled. "Mommy was talking to you."

I, then, turned my attention to Piper. "I was just saying that I was going in there to watch her play."

"Aight."

I watched them go to the playhouse and I picked up my phone to call Ashahve. After it rang three times, I ended the call. I sat there, bouncing my leg nervously, then called her again only to get the same fate. Sliding my hands down my wavy hair, I sat in the booth and watched Jordynn play while Piper cheered her on, hoping that Shavi would call me back.

❦

"What's up, shawty?"

"I don't know. You tell me," she said, then licked her lips as she looked me over.

Women were a trip. They were just as thirsty as some of these niggas out here. I looked her over, then headed to the back of the convenience store to get me some Coke for my Henny. This white wife-beater and these basketball shorts weren't hiding shit, that was for sure. When I walked back to the register, she was still standing there, talking to the clerk. I knew I was looking fresh, even in a wife-beater. My diamonds in my ears were shining, my chain was blinding their asses and my swag screamed confidence. But one more step and I swore she was gon' fuck me in this store.

I sat my Coke on the counter and shawty next to me stepped a little closer. "What's your name?"

"Rich. Yours?"

"Chenique."

I gave her a head nod. After the cashier handed me my change and wished me a goodnight, shawty was right in my face. "What's up, lil mama?"

She was aight. She ain't have shit on Ashahve or even Piper. She was on the thin side, straight up and down. Shawty didn't really have a body, but she was cute. I just wasn't attracted to her. "You want my number? Maybe we can kick it sometimes."

"Naw, shawty. I got a girl and a baby mama. I ain't tryna add no more confusion to my life. You feel me?"

"I guess, but I can be your stress reliever, Rich. Ain't no confusion coming from this way."

Females came with confusion. They got hooked to the dick and thought they owned the shit. I ain't have time for it. I was carrying my black ass back to my apartment to get fucked up by my damn self. "Well, I ain't tryna find out."

I walked out the door and got in my car as my phone rang. It was Piper. I'd let Jordynn leave with her from Chick-fil-a and I was praying that it wasn't a mistake. "Hello?"

"Hi, Da-dy! Can I stay with Mommy tonight?"

I still didn't feel great about that shit, but I said, "Yeah, baby girl. You need to come get some clothes?"

She asked her mama if she needed clothes and I heard Piper say, "Tell him yes and we will be there in about ten minutes."

"Da-dy?"

"I heard her, baby girl. I'm on my way home now."

"Okay. Bye."

"See you in a lil bit."

It was hard for me to believe that she was almost four. Her birthday would fall on the weekend before school started. Ashahve and I had been trying to brainstorm about what type of party we would give her, but now it seemed that would all be up to me. I didn't really have any family that I knew of, besides my cousin. So, I'd probably just end up taking her to Jumping World or somewhere like that.

After I parked in my spot, at the apartment complex, and was getting out, Piper drove through the gate and parked next to me. Jordynn ran to me, excitedly, as I stood there waiting for them. "Da-dy, me and Mommy are gonna be queen and princess."

"Who's gon' be the queen and who's gon' be the princess?"

"Well, I'm the girl, so I have to be the princess."

"Oh, okay. I thought you were the queen, since you're the boss."

She frowned and actually looked like she was thinking about it until Piper and I laughed. I unlocked the door and she and Piper went to her room to get clothes. I plopped down on my couch and turned on the TV while I listened to Jordynn boss Piper around, telling her what to pack. I shook my head slowly, as I chuckled to myself. When they emerged, Piper was carrying two duffle bags. I frowned, but before I could ask why in the hell she needed two duffle bags, she opened one to reveal Jordynn's dolls and stroller.

"She couldn't leave these behind. She had to have her babies, or they were gonna cry without her." She rolled her eyes. "Rich, if it's okay, I packed her a couple of extra changes of clothes to keep at my house."

"That's fine, Piper. Be good, baby girl. I'll see you tomorrow, okay?"

"Okay, Da-dy! You gon' call Shavi?"

"Yep."

She smiled brightly. Piper didn't need to know my business, but I was almost sure that Jordynn would tell her every detail as soon as they got out of my sight. "I love you, Da-dy."

"I love you too, munchkin."

"See you tomorrow."

"Aight, Piper."

I opened the door for them and watched them get in the car. As they drove away, Jordynn waved at me, with a huge smile on her face.

For the first time, in a long ass time, I would have the house to myself. I closed the door and locked up, then poured my Coke and Henny. My phone chimed, alerting me of a text message. It was Mali. *Can I come over?*

I thought about it for a moment, then decided against it. *Naw, I'm gon' chill tonight, baby girl.*

Technically, Ashahve and I were still together. I only told her I would bring her things. We never said we would be going our separate ways. Although my actions implied that, I hadn't let her go. After sitting the bottle of Henny and the bottle of Coke on the coffee table, I sat on the couch and downed my drink. Immediately I poured another one and did the same thing. I planned to hit the reset button by getting fucked up tonight. I'd start over tomorrow.

🕸 10 🕸

E lijah

I sat in Sertino's Café eating a sandwich and drinking a smoothie, watching the cars pass through the parking lot of the shopping strip. Today had been a long day of nothingness. I'd tried calling Nyera, but she never picked up the phone. I guess she was done like she said she would be. I didn't want to give up on her after what Ashahve had told me about her past abusive relationship, but she didn't leave me a choice, if she wouldn't answer the phone.

I'd had to get my hand looked at, because it was still swollen, the day after I'd punched the wall. It had a sprain that caused the swelling, so I had to wrap it. It was feeling pretty good now, so I hadn't been wearing the bandage. I was just sure not to put too much pressure on it, handling it tenderly, until it was closer to being one hundred percent better.

Just as I was about to head home for the evening, it felt like God had smiled on me. Ashahve had walked in with a bag on her shoulder. She ordered some type of drink, then sat in a far corner of the café. I dumped my trash in the receptacle, then walked over to her table. When she looked up and saw me, she smiled. "Dr. Coleman. How are you?"

"I'm great, Ms. Glasper. How are you?"

I looked her over and noticed she looked extremely fatigued. Her eyes were somewhat puffy, and she looked like she hadn't slept last night. She looked down in her lap. "It seems it's the season for breakups. Omari broke up with me yesterday."

"I'm so sorry. What happened?"

"Someone sent me a picture of him holding a woman's hand at his job. I sent the picture to him and when he tried to explain, I kind of went off on him. I was angry. The picture looked so incriminating. He told me the woman had flirted with him after he'd fixed her tire, but he declined her advances. I didn't believe him. So, in so many words, he told me he didn't have time to deal with bullshit and if I didn't trust him, then we didn't need to be together."

I took a deep breath. That picture was circumstantial at best. "Has he ever given you a reason to doubt his loyalty to you? Or a reason not to trust him?"

"No."

"Then, why don't you? Why can't you believe he's telling the truth about what happened?"

"Because every man I've dated has cheated on me. Seeing that picture made me believe that he would be capable of that, too. I don't want to be hurt, Elijah," she said softly.

"Listen. There's nothing I want more than to have another chance with you. But... you have to give him the benefit of the doubt. Your past has nothing to do with him. Just like Nyera's past has nothing to do with me. You have to give him a chance, Ashahve. What if he passed by here and saw you talking to me? This is completely innocent, but because of our past, he could assume that we're seeing one another again."

"You're right. You're so right." She reached across the table and grabbed my hand. "Thank you."

It felt like every nerve in my body had responded to her touch. She slid her hand from mine, as I stood. I smiled at her. "It was good to see you, Ashahve."

"It was good to see you, too."

I forced my legs to walk away. I could have sat there with her for eternity. Although my mind was kicking me in the ass for defending Omari. Now that I had dated her cousin, there was no way I could openly date Ashahve without it looking like we'd stabbed Nyera in the back. However, nothing could stop us from messing around again, if we wanted to. Just the thought of pleasing her body again had my dick straining against my zipper.

What I wouldn't give to taste her again... hold her in my arms... kiss her... make love to her. She was my weakness and to see her hurting made it hard for me to refrain from consoling her. As I got to my car, I got a text from her. I looked back toward the café, with a slight frown, then got in my car to read what she'd sent. *Can I come over?*

Oh, my Lord. That probably wouldn't be a good thing. If she came over, I was gonna want to make love to her. She probably felt like she had a friend in me, right now. *Where was Tia or Nyera?* Why did she wanna come to my house? As if reading my thoughts, she texted again. *Tia is at work and Nyera went to Longview for the weekend. My mama and daddy are having a date night and my brother is in the wind, as usual. Please?*

I closed my eyes and took a few deep breaths. Could I handle being alone with her? Probably not, but I responded in the affirmative anyway. *Sure.*

I started my engine and headed home to wait for her. My heart was racing, and my mind was all over the place, trying to figure out how I would keep my dick in check. If I thought she was gonna take longer, I would have run on the treadmill to exert some energy. Despite how tired she looked, she was beautiful in her gray jogging pants and lime and gray top. The way they stretched over her ass and around her hips had me salivating.

As I sat watching TV, there was a light knock at the back door. When I got to it, I saw that she'd driven her car around to the back of the house, where it couldn't be seen from the street. I opened the door and stepped aside for her to come in. She went straight to the sofa and flopped down, taking off her lime green and gray tennis shoes. I sat next to her and she leaned against me as she tucked her feet under her body. "Did you call him?"

"No. It's like I can't make myself do it."

"Why not? Has he called you?"

"Yeah. A few times."

"So, what's the problem?"

"I'm scared."

"Ashahve, look at me."

She lifted her head and stared into my eyes. I closed mine, briefly, then stared back into her sad but beautiful, brown eyes. "You're heartbroken, now and most likely, he hasn't done anything wrong. You're putting yourself through heartache for nothing."

She laid her head on my shoulder and started to cry. *Oh, God, help me.* I lifted my arm and wrapped it around her, allowing her to cry into my chest. Gently pushing her hair from her face, I kissed the top of her head. Closing my eyes, I did my best to talk my dick down as she wrapped her arms around my neck. After a moment, she quickly pulled away, then swallowed hard enough for me to notice. "I'm sorry, Dr. Coleman."

"Ashahve. Quit tripping. In this house, I'm always Elijah. You know that."

She blushed, then laid her head on my shoulder. I laid back on the sofa, then put my arm around her once again. The problem came when she stared up at me. Trying to keep my gaze straight ahead, I ended up yielding to temptation. I looked down at her, then leaned over and kissed those pretty lips. She was receptive. Shavi held my face in her hands and took ownership of what was already hers. I slid my tongue in her mouth, kissing her the way I remembered she liked to be kissed as my hands slid down her back to her ass.

Slowly I pulled away from her. She was vulnerable and I was taking advantage. This wasn't right and I knew she would regret every moment of this, especially if she and Omari made up. As if reading my thoughts, once again, she laid her head on my chest and I laid back on the sofa. I didn't want to just be her friend but, at this moment, I would be whatever she needed me to be, just to be in her presence. Slowly stroking her hair, I could feel her body become more relaxed. I rested my hand on her hip and closed my eyes.

❦

WHEN I WOKE UP, the sun was shining through the window. I was laying on my back, on the sofa, and Ashahve was on top of me, her head laying on my chest. Her phone was vibrating like crazy in her pocket. "Shavi?"

She lifted her head, then jumped up. "Oh, goodness. What time is it?"

"It's nearly seven. We both fell asleep."

"Shit. My mama is probably worried sick."

"Your phone was vibrating right before I woke you up."

She looked at it, then rolled her eyes. I assumed that wasn't her mother. "I'm sorry, Elijah, for taking up your whole night. Thank you for everything."

She walked closer to me and hugged me tightly, then kissed my lips. I walked her to the backdoor, then pulled her to me again. I hugged her tightly, then let her go. "Be careful. I'm always here for you. Okay?"

"Thanks."

With that, she headed out the door. Although she was hurting, last night was amazing. I missed holding her in my arms and kissing those soft lips. As hard as I was trying to keep my heart out of it, it was opening up to her anyway. I couldn't help it. I still loved Ashahve

Glasper. But I would do anything to make her happy, even if that meant helping her heal to go back to him.

I sat on the sofa and shook my head slowly, realizing how bad I had it. Usher had the shit right when he sang about it nearly twenty years ago. Making love to her was all I could think about, but I was proud of myself for sacrificing my needs for her. She wouldn't have blamed me for it, but I didn't want her to be angry with herself either. Sometimes, she was extremely hard on herself and I understood that. I was the same way. But talking to my counselor had helped me put things into perspective.

Things happened beyond our control, sometimes. Even if something happened that was within our control, we couldn't always dwell on it. Most times, there was nothing we, as people, could do to rectify what had happened. Learn from it, get over it, let it go and move on. I was happy with where I was in my life and I refused to miss a day taking my medication. I felt renewed and like I was in a good place, spiritually.

I stood from my seat to go brush my teeth and take a quick run on my treadmill. Before I could get on the treadmill, I got a call and my eyes widened for a moment. I didn't expect her to ever call me again. It was Nyera. "Hello?"

"Hi, Elijah."

"Hey."

"I just wanted to apologize for the way I left." She exhaled loudly, then continued. "My last relationship was horrible. When you told me about your ex and you assaulting her, it brought back some horrible memories for me, that I couldn't handle. I'm a victim of domestic abuse and he literally almost killed me. I got scared. He started off sweet and gentle, but after we were together for a few months, close to a year, the abuse started. I can't go through that again."

"I understand, Nyera. My situation with my ex was out of character for me. Our relationship was nothing like that. That was the only instance that had happened, and it was like I snapped when I found out what she was doing to me. I didn't go there to assault her, but when she acted like she was proud of what she did, and was so unapologetic, I lost it. I'm sorry that brought back unpleasant memories for you."

"Thank you for being so understanding. I came home for a little while to clear my head, but I'm about to head back to Beaumont in a little bit. Can I take you to dinner when I get back?"

"Sure. Just call me when you get back."

"I still don't think I can have a relationship, right now, but I do want to still see you. Is that okay?"

"Yeah."

Another friend. Was God punishing me or what? I slowly shook my head at the predicaments I was in. I was too soft-hearted to deny either of them. Although I wasn't in love with Nyera, I did care for her. "Okay. I'll call you later."

"Okay. Be careful. That's a long drive."

"Yeah. Almost four hours. But I'm good with it. I jam the whole way."

I chuckled. "Okay. I look forward to your call."

"Okay. Bye."

Soft-ass Elijah. Felt like I was a damn counselor. I needed to get paid for my services. Having a degree in psychology along with my sociology degree was beneficial to me. It helped me understand life a little better from all aspects. While there were always things that I knew I would never understand, I could handle them better by seeing the arguments from all points of view.

I got on the treadmill and took my run, letting my mind run wild with how I could easily get caught up again, if I wasn't careful.

Omari

"WHERE THE FUCK are you with my baby? You asked for another night and now it's nine o'clock Sunday night. She starts her new daycare tomorrow."

"She's my baby, too, Rich. I'm keeping her and ain't shit you can do about it."

"That's where you're wrong. I filed abandonment charges on your ass. Now, bring my baby back before I call the police, Piper."

"Call them. Good luck with them finding me."

She ended the call and I immediately hopped in the car to fly to her house. I didn't know what the fuck she was on, but I couldn't live without my baby. When everything else went wrong, I had Jordynn. She always loved me, and I did nothing wrong in her eyes. I needed Jordynn as much as she needed me. That bitch couldn't have my baby. A tear had fallen from my eye and I quickly swiped it. She found a way to bring me to my knees.

When I got there, I didn't see her car. I ran up on the porch and banged on the door, only to not get a response. Backing away, I ran back to the door and knocked that shit off the hinges. Fuck! They were gone. I paced back and forth and let the hurt, worry and anger consume me. Jordynn was all I had in this world and that bitch was fucking with my life. Jordynn was my life! Before leaving, I tore that fucking house up, looking for a clue to lead me to them. That was all for naught, because I didn't find shit to lead me to my baby.

I left the house with her favorite shirt in my hand. I bought it a couple of weeks ago. When I got in my car, I put her shirt to my face, smelling her lotion scent in it. Before I could stop it, I broke down, crying in that shirt. At this point, I would do anything to get my baby back. Nothing was off limits. I dried my face with it, then threw it to the passenger seat and drove back home. I called the police to report her for kidnapping.

Of course, she couldn't kidnap her own child, but since I'd filed the abandonment charge, maybe they would do something to help me get my baby back. I'd also released Jordynn to her, so it was a toss-up. I sat on my couch, praying that Piper would have a change of heart and bring my baby back. I'd drank myself into a stupor Friday night and didn't wake up until almost noon, Saturday. That afternoon, Piper and Jordynn had called to see if she could stay another night. I'd agreed but told Piper to have Jordynn back by six, so I could get her ready for bed.

I started calling her ass at six thirty to see what was going on and she apologized and said she was running late because she'd brought 'Tutu' to a family barbeque. I'd accepted that and told her to get her home as soon as she could, because I had to be to work at eight and had to bring Jordynn to daycare before that. I started calling again at eight and she wouldn't answer the fucking phone. Beating myself up for even letting her spend the night, my phone started ringing. I quickly grabbed it from the coffee table to see Ashahve calling me.

I couldn't talk to her right now. My nerves were on one and I needed to calm down first. I didn't want to go off on her for how I was feeling about Piper. The only thing I could imagine was choking the fuck out of that bitch. There was a knock at the door, and I knew it was probably the police to file my report. When I opened the door, they introduced themselves and I allowed them in my spot. We all sat at the table, as one of them took out a form. "So, Mr. Watson, can you tell me what happened, starting with Friday?"

After telling them everything, starting with the abandonment charges I'd had filed against her to what she said in our last phone conversation, the female officer looked at me with sympathetic eyes. I gave them the type of car she had and pictures of the both of them. "I'm sorry this is happening to you, Mr. Watson. You could possibly have a case of parental kidnapping. Since you filed the abandonment charges, it left you being the custodial parent. I'm not a lawyer and I could be wrong, but the district attorney will be in touch with you. This has been an ongoing problem in this area, and he wants to handle these cases, no matter how complicated they may be."

"Thank you. I need my baby back," I replied, getting a little choked up.

"In the meantime, we will be looking for her," the male officer informed me.

I nodded, then stood from the table and walked them to the door. Once they left, I realized I didn't need to be alone. The only person I wanted here with me was Ashahve. I grabbed my phone and called her. She answered on the first ring. "Omari?"

"Hey. Can you come over? I know it's late, but I need you."

"What's going on?"

"We'll talk about it when you get here. I'm sorry for pushing you away."

"I'm sorry, too. I'm on my way."

I ended the call and headed to the kitchen to fix me a drink. My job would be a thing of the past until I got my baby back. I'd be done fucked somebody car up while thinking about my baby. I knew she missed me, and I wondered what Piper was trying to fill her mind with. The more I thought about that bitch, the angrier I got. I swore, if I found her before the police did, I was gon' fuck her up on sight. My baby would have to go to counseling and everything when I finished with her ass.

I didn't like the nigga she was bringing back to the forefront. The mutha-fucka that shot first and asked questions later.

The bastard that could snap your neck with little effort.

The jackass that could verbally annihilate you.

The cold-ass nigga that wouldn't piss on you if you were on fire.

He was here and would probably be here to stay, until I got my baby back. The knock at my door brought me back from my thoughts... my visions of Piper in a fucking casket. Going to the door, I swung it open and walked away. Ashahve timidly walked in and closed it behind her. I turned to her and said, "That bitch took my baby."

"What?"

"You heard me. Piper took my fucking daughter, and I don't know where they are."

My lip twitched from the anger coursing through me, then quivered like I was about to cry. Ashahve ran to me and hugged me tightly, while I stood there, still reeling from tonight's revelation. I couldn't hug her back or show much affection, because the only person I wanted to show affection to, at the moment, was Jordynn. "My God, Omari. I'm so sorry. How did she get her?"

I broke away from her and sat on the sofa. "She called wanting to see Jordynn, Friday. We went to Chick-fil-a and they were having such a great time together. She and Jordynn asked if Jordynn could spend the night with her. I said okay. They came and got clothes and I haven't seen my baby since."

Ashahve grabbed my hand and held it in hers, gently stroking it. The affection I didn't think I wanted to give her was bubbling in my chest. "What are the police doing, baby?"

"The district attorney is supposed to call me tomorrow. In the meantime, they are looking for her. I gave them pictures." I took a deep breath. "Ashahve, listen. I'm sorry..."

"Shh. Don't worry about that right now. I love you, Omari, and I know you love me. Let's just forget about that."

I lifted my arm and pulled her close to me. We sat there in silence, for a while, until I led her to my bedroom. I got on my knees and Ashahve joined me. "Lord, please... I know I'm not the best guy in the world, but my baby makes me better. Please bring her back to me, unharmed. Whatever I need to do, I'll do it. I'm gon' die without my baby. She's my life. Please..."

The tears fell from my closed eyes and I could feel Ashahve wiping them away. Standing to my feet, I laid in the bed and Shavi laid next to me, pulling me in her arms. She rubbed the back of my head as I laid on her chest and wrapped my arms around her waist. I was drained, but I knew I wouldn't be sleeping tonight. Not without at least knowing where my daughter was and that she was safe.

Breathing deeply, I was trying to stay relaxed, but that shit was impossible. I had a headache from hell and all I wanted to do was find my way to my baby. First thing in the morning, I would go to Piper's mother's house. She had to know where she'd gone with my baby. If she didn't know, I wouldn't have a choice but to wait on the police and detectives to do their jobs. "Omari?"

"Yeah?"

"I know you probably don't wanna talk, but I just want you to know that I'm gonna take a leave of absence from my job. I need to be here with you. I love Jordynn, too, and this is hard to believe. I do believe that God will bring her back to you... to us. My mama started screaming when I told her. My parents love Jordynn like she's their grandbaby. Whatever you need from me or them, we're here for you, baby."

"Thank you, Shavi."

While her words were filled with love, I felt no relief. My daughter was gone. The thought of never seeing her again was only fueling my rage... heightening the hurt I felt. I hated the way I was feeling right now. So many emotions were flowing through my body, at once, I didn't know how I would function. Ashahve kissed my head and I could hear her whispering. She was praying for me and Jordynn. I even heard her mention Piper in her prayers.

I hoped she'd prayed that I didn't break Piper's fucking neck.

A shahve

I'D BEEN SPENDING every day, all day, with Omari. Jordynn had been gone for a week and I could see him slowly losing it. I was so glad he'd called me. However, when he did, I immediately felt bad about running to Elijah's arms. Omari had been ignoring my calls and, after Friday morning, I thought we were done. If he ever found out I did that, he would be done. I was so vulnerable, and he was the only person that was available that I knew I could talk to. I wasn't expecting things would go as far as they did. My ass should've stayed at home.

Omari and I had gone to Piper's mother's house and I thought she would have an attitude with Omari. However, she was just the opposite. She hugged him tightly and apologized over and over while crying. The relationship they shared was touching and it had tears streaming down my cheeks. He introduced us and she apologized to me as well, then promised if she heard anything from Piper, she would let him know.

So, this week has been filled with constant anguish, driving around, aimlessly, in search of Jordynn and Piper. Omari was convinced that she could be hiding in plain sight, making everyone think that she'd skipped town. We'd checked every hotel and motel in all of the Golden Triangle. When we weren't driving around, we were waiting with the phones in our hands, hoping someone would call with good news.

Today was no different. We were at Omari's apartment, on the sofa, letting the TV watch us. The detective had called yesterday to tell us they still had no leads. I could literally see the life leaving Omari's body, little by little, every day he had to go without Jordynn. It was so sad to watch. The man that was so full of life, cracking jokes at every turn and always saying and doing whatever was on his mind, was now quiet, saddened and filled with rage. It didn't take much to set him off and I understood.

Yesterday, after the detective had called, he'd snapped on me because I'd fixed him a sandwich. He yelled and said, *Did I ask for something to eat?* The way he looked at me had scared me something fierce. I had to walk on eggshells around him and I hated every minute of it. I didn't like feeling scared of him. While he was hurting, that shit was pushing me away. It was making me not want to be around him. I didn't know if I would eventually do something to set him off.

My phone rang, breaking me from my thoughts as Omari laid on my lap. He sat up so I could answer it. "It's Nyera."

He laid back on my lap, without a word, as I answered. "Hello?"

"Hey."

"Hey, girl. What's up?"

"Not too much. I was calling to check to see if any progress had been made."

"No. Nothing yet. We haven't lost hope, though."

"Well, no. We can't lose hope. I believe she's okay and that, eventually, something will shake loose, revealing their whereabouts."

"Yeah. Me, too, cuz. Me, too."

"Y'all want something to eat?"

"No. I cooked."

"See if she could bring a pizza. I'm not really feeling what you cooked," Omari said.

My heart dropped as he stood from the sofa and went outside. "It's not you, Ashahve. What kind of pizza does he like?"

I sucked up my emotions. "He usually eats pepperoni with Jordynn."

"Okay. I'll be there in thirty minutes."

"Thanks."

I closed my eyes and took a deep breath. Jordynn being gone was taking a toll on him, but it was taking a toll on me, too. I missed her, but I missed him, too. This person he'd become was someone I didn't wanna deal with. I didn't know how long I would be able to stomach him. Laying on the sofa, I glanced at the spaghetti and garlic toast on the stove and contemplated throwing it all out, but then I knew that would start an argument. Maybe, after Nyera left, I would get out of here for a little while. I needed to rejuvenate my damn self.

I went to the room and put on more presentable clothing as I heard the door close. Omari had come back inside. As I slid on my jeans, he appeared in the doorway. "Where are you going?"

"After Nyera leaves, I was gonna get out for a little bit."

He gave me a head nod, then walked away. I needed my man back, but I knew, until we found Jordynn, he would be absent. I slid on a tank top and my sandals, then went back to the front. Omari looked me from head to toe as I sat next to him. "I guess you need a break from me, huh?"

"It's not that."

"Yeah, it is. It's okay, though. I need a break from me, too."

My heart dropped as I kissed his cheek. He roughly threw me to the couch and laid on top of me. My heart was beating rapidly. He'd scared the fuck out of me. We hadn't had sex since I'd gotten here a week ago. Omari lifted his shirt over his head and began roughly removing my clothes. I grabbed his head as he lifted my bra, pinching my nipple between his lips. Hissing through the pain and pleasure, I lifted my hips into him.

Unbuttoning my pants and yanking them down with my underwear, Omari pulled out his dick and shoved himself inside of me. That shit hurt so good, I couldn't help but scream in response. He grunted loudly, then growled out, "This my shit, Shavi?"

"Yeah, baby! Shit!"

I could feel that shit in my abdomen and back. Omari was fucking me up for real. This was his way of making sure I didn't leave. After this, I wouldn't be able to. He went up on his knees and lifted my hips, slamming me onto him. "Omaariiiii! Fuck!"

"Take this dick, Shavi. Quit tryna run from the shit."

He sounded so damn calm when he said that, it was an eerie feeling. How could he be ripping me to shreds and be so calm about it? He'd zoned out. "Omari... look at me, baby."

His eyes focused on me, and I could see the sorrow in them. I held his face in my hands as he lessened the impact of his assault. Shortly after, he nutted deep inside of me. I pulled his face to mine and kissed him with as much passion as I could muster. He was so broken. After letting his tongue dance with mine for a moment, he quickly pulled away, leaving me laying there half-naked, without a word. When he came back, he had a wet towel and wiped my snatch, then walked away again. I pulled my underwear and pants up, as the doorbell rang.

I was pretty sure that was Nyera. I pulled my bra over my breasts, then fixed my tank and went to the door. It wasn't Nyera. "Omari! It's the detective!"

I opened the door, and when I saw the solemn expression on his face, my heart dropped. Omari ran to the front, in his shorts only, then froze. "We need to move quickly. They are both in Hermann Memorial Hospital in Houston. There was an accident."

"Fuck!" Omari yelled, scaring the hell out of me.

I slipped my sandals on and went to the back to comb my hair as Omari put on some jeans and a shirt with his Js. As we were running to the front, the detective slowed us down. "I don't know what we will see, but I need you to try to contain your rage when we get there."

Omari nodded and damn near pushed his ass out the apartment. "Shavi, I don't think you should come."

"What?" I asked, my eyes wide.

"I don't think you should come."

"Omari, why not?"

"I don't want to have to deal with both of our emotions. Plus, I don't want you to witness what might happen to Piper's ass."

"Omari... please don't do this."

"Go home, shawty. I'll call you when I get back."

He jumped in his car and took off after the cop, while I stood there in shock. My heart was crumbling in my chest. I slowly walked back to his apartment while the tears streamed down my cheeks. Sitting on the couch, I called my job and let them know that they could put me back on the schedule. I was so hurt, I couldn't think straight. The knock at the door caught me off guard. I jumped off the sofa, hoping he'd come back for me. When I saw Nyera, I burst into tears. "Shavi! What's wrong?" she asked as she walked inside with the large pepperoni pizza.

I walked back to the sofa and flopped on it, bringing my hands to my face. "He left me! The detective came and said that they found Jordynn and Piper in Houston. They'd gotten in a car accident. He made me stay here!"

"What? Why?"

"He didn't want to have to deal with my emotions along with his."

She sat next to me and pulled me in her arms. This whole situation was fucked up. Jordynn could be hurt, or worse, and all Omari could think about was himself. How could I be there for him or

Jordynn if he pushed me away? I sat there for a little while longer, then stood from the sofa and went to the bedroom. Dragging my duffle bag from the closet, I packed all my clothes while Nyera watched. "I'll go put the food away."

I nodded my head. My head was hurting, along with my heart. I still couldn't believe he left me. I'd been here for him all week, letting him talk to me however he wanted to talk to me, only to be treated like a random bitch today. He fucked me to get a nut, not allowing his feelings to be present and the moment they were trying to present themselves, he nutted. Then, he sent me away, saying he'd call me, like I was just a fuck. That shit hurt.

When I got back up front, Nyera had put the food away and cleaned the kitchen. She gave me a look of sympathy. "You wanna come to my place?"

"No. I'm gonna go home. I'll call you later. Thanks."

She smiled softly, then hugged me tightly. When she released me, I took Omari's key off my ring. I played with it in my hand, for a moment, as more tears left me. We walked out the door and, after locking it, I put the key under his doormat. Nyera hugged me again and we walked to our cars. When I got inside and had cranked up, I changed the station to soul town. The older songs always helped me through whatever I was going through. However, when "Ain't No Way" by Aretha Franklin came on, I literally wailed.

After pulling myself together, I headed home, praying that Jordynn was okay.

O mari

"Daddy's here, baby girl."

"Hi, Da-dyyy," Jordynn whined.

When I saw my baby, I nearly lost it, trying to get to her. Piper was in ICU. Lucky for her. She had a better chance there than being anywhere near me. My baby had a broken leg. They'd been t-boned when Piper ran a stop sign. Thank God they got hit on her side and not Jordynn's. That would have killed her. She had some cuts and bruises, but nothing she wouldn't heal from. Her leg was in a cast and she had a laceration on her arm that had required stitches.

The doctor told me they'd put her to sleep to reset her leg and had been giving her pain injections every six hours. Sitting next to her in her bed, she laid her head on my arm. "I missed you, Da-dy."

"I missed you, too, baby. So much."

I kissed the top of her head and thought about Ashahve. Not knowing what I would get here and find had me so in my feelings, I lashed out at her. I'd been making it hard for her all week, and I owed her an apology. I just hoped she accepted it. If I would have gotten unfavorable news, when I got here, having her with me wouldn't have been good. She would have seen a side of me that I never wanted her to see. She'd already gotten a glimpse of my weakness and the rage I felt because of it.

"Where were y'all?" I asked her.

"We went to McDonald's and Mommy's boyfriend's house."

I could feel my rage building. Who in the fuck was she dating? I barely wanted her ass around Jordynn, and she had the nerve to have another mutha-fucka around my baby? "Where was he when y'all got in the wreck?"

"He was in the car, too, but he got out and ran."

What the fuck? Piper had swelling on her brain and probably wouldn't even remember this shit. My baby was left with all the horrible memories. I could feel my rage building and I wanted to go find that fucker. "What's his name?"

"I don't remember."

I could tell she was lying. My baby never lied to me. That made me wonder why she was lying. "Look at Daddy, baby girl." When she looked up at me with her big brown eyes, I continued. "You can always talk to me. No matter what it is and no matter who told you not to say anything. Daddy will always do his best to protect you. You understand?"

"Yes," she said as she looked away.

"What happened, baby? What's his name?"

"Willie and Mommy was fussing. I covered my ears, 'cause he was saying bad words."

"Were y'all with Willie the whole time you were away from me?"

"No. We were at Mommy's house. I slept in my bed twice. We just saw Willie today."

So, they'd left last Sunday. I nodded my head and put my arm around my baby. She needed to talk to a cop about this bullshit. The Beaumont Police Department was supposed to be talking to the

Houston Police Department about what happened. Piper, once she got out of here, would be prosecuted for parental kidnapping. My phone chimed letting me know I had a text message. I pulled it from my pocket to see it was from Ashahve. *Is she okay?*

I dropped my head. I felt horrible about how I treated her. *She has a broken leg and some stitches in her arm, but she's okay. Piper is in ICU.*

I was surprised she messaged me, but I knew she loved Jordynn. Now that she knew she was okay, she probably wouldn't message anymore. "Da-dy?"

"Yeah, sweetheart?"

"Where's Shavi?"

Shit. I couldn't tell her that I left her. But what else would I tell her? I didn't want to make it seem like Shavi didn't want to come. I didn't want to paint myself in a negative light either, but it was my fault that she wasn't here. "I'm sorry, baby. I was mean to her because I was so angry and worried."

"Why were you angry?"

"Because I didn't know where you were, and your mama wasn't answering the phone. I took my anger out on Shavi. I owe her an apology, because she was worried about you, too. She stayed with me, the whole week, trying to find you."

"Can I call her?"

"Well... she may not answer, because she's mad at me for leaving her."

"Please?"

I swallowed hard and called Ashahve. The phone rang a few times then went to voicemail. I ended the call and sent her a text. *Please answer. Jordynn is begging to talk to you.*

She responded quickly. *Give her the phone. I can't talk to you right now.*

I deserved that shit and more. Dialing her number, I hit send, then gave it to Jordynn. She hit the speaker phone button. "Hello?"

"Hi, Shaviiii," Jordynn whined.

"Hi, babyyyy. How are you, sweetheart?"

"I hurt my leg and my arm. A truck hit us."

"I'm so sorry that happened. I miss you."

"Can you come see me?"

"How long will you be there?"

Jordynn looked up at me. I held up one finger. The doctor had said that if everything checked out, she would be able to go home tomorrow afternoon. They'd already done a cat scan and x-rays. The only problem she had was her leg. Jordynn frowned at me. "You may go home tomorrow."

"Da-dy said I might go home tomorrow."

"Well, let me know something in the morning. If you don't go home tomorrow, I will come see you. If you get to go home tomorrow, I'll see you when you get home. Okay?"

"Okay. I miss you, too, Shavi. Willie told Mommy that he knows you."

"Willie who?"

"I don't know. He said you went to his school." *Well, ain't that some shit.* "He said he used to tease you about your name... I think."

I stood quietly, and listened, as I motioned the officers to come in the room. As they entered, Ashahve said, "Willie Clark. He used to tease me all the time. That wasn't very nice. Was it?"

"No. I told him he was mean."

"Where did you see him?"

"He was with Mommy. He left us after the truck wrecked us."

"Oooh."

I interrupted their conversation. "Baby girl, tell Shavi you'll call her tomorrow. These officers wanna talk to you."

She looked scared when she saw the cops. She whispered in the phone, "Shavi, the police are here. I hope I don't go to jail."

"I can't hear you, Jordynn. What did you say, baby?"

I took the phone from her. "Ashahve, she'll call you tomorrow. There are officers here that need to talk to her about what happened."

She didn't respond. I looked at the phone, just as she ended the call. She was serious about not talking to me. I had no one to blame but myself. It was stupid to leave her. Now that I look back on it, it was childish and selfish, too. I didn't know how I would make this up to her... make this right. The officers approached the bed with smiles on their faces. Jordynn seemed to loosen up a bit and she smiled back. "Well, hello princess. I'm Officer Mike and this is Officer Cammie. We're here to talk to you about what happened. You think you can help us figure out what went wrong?"

Jordynn looked at me, so I winked at her. She nodded. "How old are you, big girl?"

"I'm almost four, right, Da-dy?"

"That's right, baby girl. Two more weeks."

The officers smiled. "Wow! You're a big girl."

Jordynn smiled brightly. Their job of making her comfortable was a success. All she had to do, now, was tell Jordynn she was beautiful, and she would tell them anything they wanted to know. As if hearing my thoughts, Officer Cammie said, "You're such a beautiful girl. Do you know how pretty you are?"

"Yes, I do! Thank you!"

That did it. Jordynn had already reached for her hand. "Da-dy, she's nice."

I rolled my eyes as the officer laughed. She held Jordynn's hand and sat next to her. "So, that was a really bad wreck, huh?"

"Yes. Mommy and Willie were arguing and I don't think she saw that truck coming."

"Who's Willie, sweetheart? No one saw him."

"When that truck hit us, Mommy was sleep, and I was screaming 'cause my leg and arm hurt. Willie said he was going get help, but he never came back."

"Thank you, baby. You did so well. You want a sucker?"

"Yes! Thank you!"

Officer Mike pulled me off to the side while Officer Cammie kept Jordynn company. "Do you know who this Willie guy is?"

"I don't know him, but when Jordynn was on the phone with my girlfriend, she told her that he said he knew her. She identified him as Willie Clark. They went to school together. I'm assuming he's either from Beaumont or Port Arthur."

"Do you think she would be willing to talk to us about him?"

"I'm sure she would."

He handed me his card. "Please, tell her to call us at her earliest convenience, to make a statement."

I nodded and slid the card in my pocket. "Miss Jordynn?"

She looked at Officer Mike. He continued. "How did Willie know your daddy's girlfriend?"

She giggled, then put her hand over her mouth. "He said he used to tease her about her name in school. He was mean to, Shavi."

Both officers looked at me, then back at Jordynn. "You're so smart," Officer Cammie told her.

Jordynn leaned against her and smiled. It didn't take much to butter her biscuit. I'd have to keep my eyes on her. People would be able to get whatever they wanted out of her. The officers told her bye and that they would call and check on her. Jordynn was excited when Officer Cammie gave her a whistle. Could have sworn she'd gotten a million bucks. Now, she was a miniature cop. Blowing the whistle at me, telling me to halt.

I shook my head, slowly, as the officers laughed. They promised they would be in touch. Once they left, the nurse came in and put some pain medicine in Jordynn's IV. They also checked her vitals, then let us be. I took off my pants that I'd slid over my basketball shorts and got in bed with Jordynn. She laid on my shoulder. "Da-dy, can we watch Curious George?"

"Yeah, shawty."

I found the cartoon movies that were on the TV's lineup and pressed play. Before it could get through the first five minutes, she was knocked out.

❦ 14 ❦

E lijah

I'D JUST FINISHED my run on the treadmill, and I was tired as hell. Before my run, I'd lifted weights for about thirty minutes. School would be starting soon, so I had to start getting my syllabi together for the four sociology classes I would be teaching, along with the intro to psychology class, this semester. I was also teaching a graduate course in social theory. I would eventually have Ashahve in my class. When they asked me to teach it, I was overly excited.

Knowing that I'd get to teach her in graduate school was exciting. I couldn't wait to tell her. Although, I hadn't talked to her in a couple of weeks. She and Omari must have worked out their issues. More of a reason that I was glad I would be teaching this class. He would probably flip when he found out I was teaching it, but he wouldn't have a choice but to get over it. It wasn't like I begged to teach the class. I was assigned it, because I knew my shit.

Nyera had been reaching out. We went to Longhorn Steakhouse

for dinner when she got back in town, from Longview, and I enjoyed her company. We'd gone to lunch a couple of times since then and to dinner once. While I enjoyed her company and thought she was a gorgeous woman, I couldn't see us being anything more than friends. I originally thought something beautiful would have developed between us, but after that short separation, I realized she wasn't the one for me.

After taking a shower, I sat in my recliner and watched TV for a little while, then boiled me an egg with two pieces of toast. Not the best breakfast, but it would do. I wanted coffee, but my body temperature was still too high. I'd be sweating after the first sip. I brought my food back to my recliner and tuned in to Family Feud. This life of luxury would soon be ending, so I figured I'd better enjoy it. Especially since they were propositioning me to teach during the summer sessions, next year, as well.

It wasn't like I had a family or anything. At least I'd be making extra money. Teaching was something I enjoyed, especially on the college level. I didn't have to babysit anybody. The students were paying to be there. So, if they didn't listen or didn't want to come to class, that was on them. As I ate, my phone rang. I was almost sure it was my mama. She'd called last night, but I was on my way to sleep. She would have kept me awake a lot longer than I wanted to be. Grabbing my phone from the end table, I saw her name. "Hey, Mama."

"Hey. Did you go to bed early last night?"

"Yes, ma'am, I did. What are you up to?"

"Not too much. I was about to go to water aerobics, and I wanted to see if you wanted to come with me."

"Well, I don't see why not. I'm not doing anything else. What time?"

I took my phone from my ear to see it was only nine in the morning. "I usually go at one, but there's a session at eleven, if you wanna go to that one."

"Yeah, let's go at eleven. I have to go to the store later. I'm about to start meal prepping. In order to keep my spirit and mind at peace, I decided to eat cleaner. I'll only eat other things, occasionally, like when you wanna cook for me."

"Boy, please. We can go at eleven, then. How did your last appointment go?"

I briefly thought about Ashahve and how I explained to the counselor that I just couldn't seem to get her out of my system. She recommended that I not see Ashahve for an extended amount of time, but not being there when she needed me was hard. Whenever I heard her voice, even when I imagined it, it summoned me to fulfill her every need and desire. Whenever she texted, it was like I could feel her heart through her words.

Ashahve was everything to me. Letting her go... forgetting about her felt like I would be losing myself. It was like she consumed every part of me. I loved her like I'd never loved anyone, and I didn't want to stop loving her. She was everything I wanted and, had I not fucked that up, she would be with me. "My last appointment went well. They are still keeping me on the stronger dosage of medicine as a precaution, since it hasn't been that long since my uh... suicide attempt."

I hated saying the words. Just knowing I'd tried to take my own life, not once but twice within the past five years, made me feel weak as hell. It made me feel less than a man. Men handled their emotions and real men were strong and dealt with issues that arose in a manner to be admired. Men persevered through any obstacle thrown their way. As a Black man, I didn't want to be labeled as mentally ill, but that was exactly what happened.

I'd been labeled as weak and a monster at the same time. Too weak to control my emotions, but dangerous enough to harm myself or others. "What about your counseling session?"

"It went okay, Mama. I'm still having issues, but it's getting easier, as time goes by," I lied.

My mama didn't have a clue that I was still, occasionally, talking to Ashahve. It wasn't frequent, but my counselor wanted me to avoid all contact with her. The closest I'd come to that was the month or so that we didn't talk. "Well, that's good. I know when you love, you love hard. Too hard."

I sighed. "Yeah..."

"Well, let me finish cooking lunch for your daddy. You'll come pick me up?"

"Of course, Ma."

I ended the call, then went and took my medication. As I got my swim trunks and my body wash, so I could take a shower after the water aerobics class, I texted Ashahve. I hadn't heard from her in over a week. Talking to my mama about my counseling session had brought her to the forefront of my mind, even more than she already was. My mind wasn't gonna rest until I reached out in some way now. *Hey, Shavi. I just wanted to see how you were doing.*

I grabbed my satchel and put my clothes in it, along with some flip flops. When I finished, I sat back in my chair and cued up *Power*. I'd been trying to catch up on all the action I'd missed. One of my colleagues and a fellow professor at Lamar had told me how thrilling the show was. I was already on season three and I'd just started watching two weeks ago. Fully prepared to get an episode in before going to pick up my mama, I reclined my chair back and got comfortable. Just before I could hit the button on the remote to start it, my phone rang. *Ashahve.* "Hello?"

"Hi, Elijah."

"Hey. You okay," I asked as I sat up, hearing the sadness in her voice.

"I'm okay. What are you up to?"

She was lying, for whatever reason. We were usually open with one another. "I'm going to water aerobics with my mom, then I'm going to the grocery store."

"Will you be going home after that?"

"Yeah."

"Can I come over?"

"Really?"

She chuckled. "Yeah, really."

"Uh... yeah. That's fine. Um... I'll call when I get back home. Are you sure you're okay?"

"I know you can hear that I'm not okay. So, no. I'm breaking up with Omari."

"What? Why?"

"Well, it's a lot to explain. I'll talk to you about it when I get there, later on."

"Okay. I'll call you."

"Okay."

She ended the call and I sat back wondering what could have happened this time. I couldn't say that I wasn't happy, but I quickly scolded myself for rejoicing in her anguish. She was hurting, but I planned to try to ease her pain, when she got here. I'd get something to cook while I was at the store and buy her favorite flowers. She loved sunflowers. I couldn't even concentrate on *Power* after talking to her, so I decided to head to my parents' house early.

AFTER MY MAMA and I had gotten out of the pool, she said, "I'm glad you're happy, Eli. You seem so upbeat and that makes my heart smile. You've been through so much, but you just keep pushing. Although, you've stumbled along the way, who hasn't? The main thing is that you overcome. The way you've been pushing to be better, makes me proud."

I felt some type of way about her words. Even though I was pushing to be better, I wasn't trying as hard when it came to Ashahve. If she knew that, I knew she would be disappointed. Instead of disappointing her, I said, "Thanks, Ma."

We headed to the showers and I thought about calling Ashahve to tell her not to come. The thought was extremely brief, because my heart overpowered my good sense. I quickly washed up and prayed my mama did the same. The way Ashahve sounded on the phone, I was almost sure she would spend the night with me.

After drying off, moisturizing my skin and getting dressed, I headed to the front to wait for my mother. While I waited, I texted Ashahve. *My mother and I are about to leave water aerobics. I should be home in an hour.*

Okay.

I was determined to make her mine again. She wouldn't have to worry about being heartbroken. I'd take care of her physically, mentally and emotionally. Spiritually, we'd be connected through God. Nothing would stand in our way. No kids, no baby mamas, no drama. Which I didn't know if she had any of those problems, but there was always the possibility of trouble from that situation presenting itself. With me, she could live in peace. My family didn't know her, but they already liked her, just from the time they met her at the hospital.

I waited impatiently for the next ten minutes before my mama came out of there. I guess I seemed antsy, because she asked, "You okay? You seem anxious."

"I'm fine, Ma. You know I'm impatient."

"Yes, you are."

She chuckled at my admission. Once we were in the car, and I'd driven to her home, she kissed my cheek and thanked me for coming to water aerobics with her. After she got in the house, I took out of there like a bat out of hell. I wanted to get my grocery shopping done as soon as possible. Super Market Sweep wasn't gon' have nothing on how fast I would be running through that store.

I called Ashahve, on my way home, letting her know that she could come over. Her voice still sounded as sad as it did earlier, and I couldn't wait to change her tune. I'd gotten some fish to blacken and I bought broccoli to steam, along with some dinner rolls. After straightening up and starting the food, the light knock at the back door came right on time. As always, my heart rate sped up and my temperature rose in anticipation of being in her presence.

I walked to the back door and opened it to find the most beautiful woman in the world. She wore a gray crop top with some grey pants, that sort of looked like sweats, but they were tight. Glancing over her figure, I stepped aside to allow her to come inside. Once I closed the door, she fell into me and cried like she'd failed a class. "Ashahve, wow! What's going on?"

"I don't think he wants me anymore. His daughter's mother kidnapped her. When they found her, she was in the hospital and Omari wouldn't let me go with him to see about her. It's just a big ugly mess."

By the time she finished talking, she seemed so much lighter. I pulled her in my arms and caressed her back. After kissing her head, I pulled away from her. "Well, you're here now, and I'm gonna get you out of this funk. First, we're gonna eat, because I'm starving. Then, we're gonna play a few games of Uno. I have Connect Four and Dominoes, too. So, whatever it takes to put that pretty smile on your face, I'm doing."

She smiled slightly, then I kissed her forehead. She wrapped her arms around my waist. "Thank you, so much, Elijah. I'm sorry if it seems I just unload all my problems on you. Tia has been working so much, I never have time to talk to her. Some things are better said in person. It's hard discussing and talking about Omari through text."

"I understand. Come on to the table."

I led her to her seat, then went to the kitchen to fix our food. This shit was hard. Seeing her cry was bringing me down. I wanted to lead her to my bedroom and make passionate love to her, then fuck her like she liked it. What in the hell was Omari thinking? Ashahve didn't deserve this. She deserved someone to love her with everything they had. She deserved for someone to treat her like the queen that she is.

I brought our food to the table where Ashahve sat with her elbows on the table, propping her head with her hands. When she saw me, she straightened her posture. I sat a plate in front of her. "What do you want to drink?"

"Do you have tea?"

"I always have tea. Be right back."

I smiled at her, then trekked back to the kitchen for our drinks. When I came back, she was waiting with her arms stretched out on the table, palms up. Sitting our tea on the table, I sat and joined hands with her, then said grace. It was what we always did when we ate here. It brought back great memories for me. Once Ashahve took the first bite of her fish, her eyes closed, and she moaned. If my dick didn't get hard watching her, then I wasn't living. *Shit.* "Shavi, you know I still love you. So, you can't make those sounds and faces."

She blushed and smiled softly. We continued to eat and enjoy one another's company, talking and laughing about random things. When we were done, we cleaned the kitchen together, but it wasn't long before I couldn't keep my hands to myself. While she was drying the pot that we couldn't put in the dishwasher, I stood behind her and wrapped my arms around her waist. After setting the pot to the side, she spun around and wrapped her arms around my neck. *Damn.* I lowered my head and kissed her lips.

It didn't seem like we were going to be bothered with Uno, Dominoes or Connect Four. My hands slid down her back and gripped her ass. *Fuck, I missed her.* She moaned in my mouth and that set my soul on fire. I lifted her and she wrapped her legs around me. My dick was finna be home.

A shahve

"Elijah! Fuck!"

He slammed me against the wall, and I could feel my orgasm about to take me out. My legs were trembling, and I had grabbed Elijah's head, holding it to my chest as he grunted. We'd never had sex this rough and I loved every minute of it. When we first got in the room, he'd made love to me. I could tell the difference. His strokes were slow, deep and gentle. The way he stared in my eyes, as he loved me, was so overwhelming it pulled the orgasm right from me. It was like he was filling me with all the good in him.

His love.

His patience.

His understanding.

His love.

He'd eaten me out within an inch of my damn life. Had me trying to climb the damn wall, literally. His tongue was a weapon of mass destruction and, as much as I hated to admit it, I missed it. I'd came all over his tongue twice. It was like he had something to prove and I didn't mind him proving every got damn thing he wanted to prove to me sexually. Elijah had a death grip on my ass as he pumped his dick inside of me, bringing my fourth orgasm to the surface. "Shit! Shit! Shit!" I screamed.

"Fuck, Shavi! Cum for me. I'm about to cum, too, baby."

Elijah growled loudly, as he slammed into me for his final thrust. We stayed in the same position, panting and holding one another tightly. After a minute or so, he brought me to the bed and gently laid me down. He laid beside me and stroked my arm, bringing the goose-bumps to the surface. "Damn. I missed you."

I closed my eyes. I never thought I would be here again, but Omari had hurt me so badly. The tears left my eyes as I thought about how he'd called me just today. He apologized on my voicemail, but every time I heard his voice, I felt rejected by the man I loved. I couldn't handle it. Elijah wiped my cheek with his thumb. "I hope you aren't regretting what we just did. You don't have to worry. I won't be like last time. I know we can't be together because you wouldn't want Nyera to know. Just don't ignore me. Okay?"

"Okay. And I'm not regretting what we just did."

"Good."

He kissed my head, but my mind was still on Omari. I just couldn't believe he'd hurt me the way he did. I'd been there for him throughout that whole ordeal. I missed Jordynn. I was glad she was okay, but I wanted to lay eyes on her. We were supposed to be planning her party. My heart was hurting, and I'd used Elijah to make myself feel better... only, I didn't feel better. I felt worse. He pulled me in his arms and held me tightly. Kissing my neck, I slowly began blocking the thoughts of Omari from my mind and indulged in what I was feeling.

Turning to face Elijah, I kissed his lips tenderly, pulling his bottom lip into my mouth. I moaned softly as Elijah grabbed a handful of my hair, pulling my head backwards. He licked, then kissed my neck as his other hand teased my nipple. Pleasing my body had always come naturally for him, and my body enjoyed the pleasure he brought it. My orgasms seemed like they longed for him until I had sex for the first time with Omari.

Omari was the man that I thought I was made for, until last week. I practically creamed in my panties every time he looked at me. Those brown eyes touched my most sensitive parts and his thick lips brought me pleasure that had been unimaginable. But if he would be that inconsiderate of my feelings when it came to Jordynn, I wouldn't be able to handle that. Not having his attention wasn't a problem for me. I knew he was hurting.

Worried.

Angry.

However, him taking everything out on me was a lot to handle, especially when I was the one that was trying to help him through it. He didn't have anyone else who was close to him. For him to leave me, that day, felt like he'd took a knife and gutted out my insides. I didn't know if I could handle that kind of hurt again. "Shavi?"

"Yeah?"

"Look at me, baby. It seems like your mind is miles away."

"I'm sorry, Elijah."

"It's okay, baby. Let me be here for you."

I laid on his chest and exhaled while closing my eyes. Wrapping his arms around me, he laid a gentle kiss on my forehead.

ASHAHVE, please answer the phone. I fucked up. I regret that shit more than anything. You don't understand how much I miss you... how much we miss you. I need you, baby girl. Please.

I sat on my bed and cried my eyes out. In all his messages, he'd only ask me to call him back. Omari didn't bare his feelings. That wasn't his thing. So, for him to send a message like this, I knew he meant everything he said. It had been a week and Jordynn had been home for five days. Things had to be rough on him trying to take care of her alone.

Elijah had been checking on me daily. I hadn't had sex with him again. Although the last time was amazing, I knew that we weren't meant to be, and I was not only toying with his mind but toying with my emotions as well. He said he understood that I had a weak moment and that I was vulnerable, but I also knew that I'd fucked up. I shouldn't have gone to Elijah's house. I would have done better going to buy me a bottle of wine and get lit all by myself. I'd opened the door to confusion once again. I cared about Elijah and I loved him. I wasn't in love with him, though. Only one man had my heart. I just hated that he'd broken it.

After staring at my background picture on the screen of my phone, I decided to call him. In that picture, we were so happy. It felt like we had our own little family. My shaky fingers touched the icon showing his missed call from this morning. When the phone started to ring, the dormant butterflies in my stomach took flight, flapping around, uncontrollably, in my belly. "Hello?"

He answered on the first ring, and I could hear the shock and hope that filled his voice. Closing my eyes, I couldn't talk. Just to hear his voice had me so damn emotional. "Ashahve. I'm so damn sorry, baby. Thank you for calling me back."

Before I could stop them, the tears fell down my cheeks and I was crying audibly. "Fuck," he whispered. He continued softly, "I know I fucked up. Please, can I make it up to you? Please…"

"Omari…"

I broke down again. *God, why did I love him so much?* Why was this shit affecting me this badly? "Baby, please don't cry. I know I fucked up, but I promise I'm gon' make that shit up to you if you let me."

I wiped my tears, then stood from my bed and grabbed my keys from the dresser. This had to be rectified. Jordynn's birthday was tomorrow and there was no way I could let the day pass and not see her. "Omari, I'm on my way over," I said, hearing my voice quiver.

"Okay. Be careful and I'll see you when you get here."

I ended the call and slid on my flip flops. When I exited the room, I ran right into my daddy. "I'm sorry, Daddy."

"It's okay. You okay?"

"Yeah. I'm finally gonna attempt to make up with Omari."

"You sure you're ready?"

"Yes, sir."

He was so protective of me. He pulled me in his embrace and kissed my head. "Okay. Be careful. Tell Jordynn that Papa said hey."

"I will."

He smiled and went to the bathroom as I walked to the front room and out the door.

When I got to Omari's apartment complex, I wanted to throw up. My nerves were on full-throttle and I still didn't know what all I would say. As I contemplated going back home, I saw Omari step outside, from my rear-view mirror. "Now or never," I whispered to myself as I opened the door.

After getting out and closing the door, my eyes met his. Even with as hurt as I was, I felt my clit pulsate just from his sorrowful gaze. Looking everywhere but at him, I was able to cross the parking lot and make it to him without dropping a tear. However, the minute I looked up at him, he pulled me in his arms and the waterworks started. I was so damn weak around him. I thought when I saw him, especially here at his apartment complex, I would get angry all over again.

My emotions were just the opposite. I was overwhelmed with how much I'd missed him, how much I loved him, and how much I just wanted to be near him. As I laid my head on his chest, he kissed it. "Come inside, baby, so we can talk."

I pulled away from him and nodded, then followed him through the door. The place smelled amazing, like he'd been cleaning up all day and I could also smell the faint scent of seafood. Omari and Jordynn loved fish and shrimp. They had one of them at least once a week, sometimes both. He closed the door and grabbed my hand, leading me to the couch. "Where's Jordynn?"

"She's in her room, asleep."

After we'd sat for a minute or so in silence, Omari began. "I'm so sorry I hurt you, Shavi. You were there for me, putting up with my shitty attitude, overbearing demands and plain ol' disrespect. How you did it still baffles me. Then, I treated you like you weren't the one I needed the most. I broke your heart when I made it seem like you didn't matter. That was fucked up. It was cold, heartless, inconsiderate and selfish. I love you, so much, Shavi."

I swallowed the lump in my throat as I did my best to hold the tears in. Omari's aura was swallowing me whole. "This was so hard for me. It still is. I love you, too, and that's why this shit is killing me. It's hard for me to understand how you could treat me the way you did, without feeling a way about it. Every day, that week, I seemed to get torn down until I barely had anything left to give. Omari, you made me feel like I was insignificant in your life. I never want to feel that way again."

"Shavi, I promise, if you give me another chance, I will show you how much you deserve to be treated like a queen. I want to show you that I can be the man you need. This shit is hard for me, too. I'm not used to anybody being there for me. I lost that shit a few years ago. She was the only woman that knew what made me tick. We've gotten so close and, even as the woman I love, I know you don't know as much about me as you should. That's my fault. There are things that I have a hard time with, and I plan to eventually tell you. I just can't go there right now."

"Da-dy!"

Hearing Jordynn's voice put a slight smile on my face. Omari stood from the couch and went to the kitchen. I sat there playing with my nails, still trying to figure out what I would say. "Shavi?"

"Yeah?"

"You wanna come in the room with me?"

He stood at the end of the hallway, holding a glass of orange juice and some medicine. I nodded, then stood and followed him to her room. "Shawty, you got company," Omari said to Jordynn when he entered her room.

"Who?"

When I walked in, she screamed. I flinched slightly, then laughed. However, when I looked over her little body, I saddened a bit. Her leg was in a cast, and I could see the scratches on her face. I went to her and hugged her tightly. Before I could get away, she struggled to scoot over in the bed. I got in with her and said, "I hate you're in pain."

"Me, too, Shavi. Look my arm."

I was no longer Mommy in her life, so she'd gone back to calling me Shavi. That didn't bother me, because I wasn't really ready for her to call me that in the first place. I looked at the huge cut, then kissed her head. "I'm sorry, baby girl."

"Can you stay in here with me?"

"Of course."

After she drank her orange juice and had taken her medicine, she laid in my arms. I caressed her like she was my baby that I'd birthed. I loved this little girl and, even if Omari and I didn't work out, I needed to always be in her life.

Once she'd fallen asleep, I went back to the front with Omari. He was watching TV. When I sat next to him, he turned to me and grabbed my hand. I felt so damn uncomfortable because I had been with Elijah. I'd fucked up, too, even though I thought that we were over. I should have given myself more time before going there with anyone, let alone Elijah. "Please tell me you forgive me."

"I do," I said lowering my head. "But we can't just pick up where we left off. Not until you feel comfortable telling me every-thing I need to know. I can't fully understand you and the things that you do if I don't know the underlying cause. I love you, Omari, and I want to be with you, but I can't let you just walk all over me because of something else going on in your life. Remember how you chewed my ass out when I took you to lunch that day? You went off on me because I was tired as hell and not talking much to you."

He smirked. He knew exactly where I was going with this. Omari didn't talk to me for over a week, because he was pissed. "I remember and I understand. Maybe one day, Jordynn can spend time with your parents, and we can talk."

"Okay. So, what are y'all doing for her birthday tomorrow?"

"Well, I thought we could come over and eat cake and ice cream. We can't do much of anything else with her leg in that cast."

"Let me make sure my parents don't have plans. If they don't, we can all come over here, so you don't have to bring her out."

He nodded, then smiled at me and pulled me closer. "I'm really glad you came over. I missed you."

I hugged him around his neck. I'd missed him, too, which was why I had to come over. After pulling away, he kissed me lightly on my lips. My insides were melting from his touch, and I knew I had to get out of there. "Are we a couple again? I had a feeling that you'd broken up with me. We haven't talked in over a week."

"Not until we can talk again. Okay?"

"That's fair."

"I'm gonna go. I need to go find Jordynn a birthday gift. I just had to come here first. I needed to see her."

"Oh. She was the only one you needed to see, Shavi?"

His eyes were staring through to my heart. Why did matters of the heart have to be so damn difficult? "I needed to see you, too."

"Damn, I need you, girl."

My first thought was, *Oh, now you need me? You didn't need me in Houston, though.* I let my pettiness stay on the inside, though, because clearly there was more to him that I didn't know about. He roughly pulled my body to him and squeezed my ass. *God, help me.* He was turning me on so much. I really needed to get out of there. When I tried to pull away, he held me tighter. "Omari, I have to go."

"No, you don't. You wanna go, because I do shit to yo' body that you can't control. Let me scratch that itch for you."

"Omari..."

"Naw, Shavi." He leaned in close to my ear and said, "I know that pussy wet. Let me have a conversation with her."

Fuck, nigga. My shit was juicing all in my panties and my breathing was so shallow, I was damn near dead. *Don't fold, Shavi!* Then he kissed my neck and nibbled on my earlobe. *Shit!* The moan escaped my lips and the minute it did, he scooped me up in his arms and brought me to his bedroom. *No!* That's what my mind was saying, but my body was saying, *Fuck me, daddy!* When we got to his room, he threw me to the bed. "You know you want this big mutha-fucka," he said, grabbing his dick after closing and locking the door.

My shit felt like it wanted to squirt on his ass as I laid there watching him. He dropped his shorts and that beautiful sight before my eyes made my lips part. I got on my hands and knees and crawled to the end of the bed as my mouth watered. I loved his dick and he knew that. He walked closer to me and rubbed the head of his dick from my forehead, down my nose to my lips. I immediately slurped that shit in my mouth and sucked it like it would be the last time.

He grabbed my head and fucked my mouth, causing me to gag, leaving that slick, thick saliva all over him. "Damn, Shavi. Swallow this dick, shawty."

I thought I was imagining things when I felt the wetness between my legs. Just his words had made me squirt all over his bed. I was so turned on, there was no turning back now. When that happened, he yanked me up and flipped me over. Shortly after, his dick was tearing my cervix to shreds and I had to bury my face in the bed to muffle my screams. Omari wasn't the least bit concerned with how I was trying to get away from him. He only held me tighter and fucked me up. "This shit mine, shawty. And I don't appreciate you giving it away."

My head snapped up. How the fuck did he know I slept with someone else? Did he follow me to Elijah's? I tried to look back at him, but he smashed my head to the bed and straddled me. "Yeah, I know you slept with somebody. I can tell by the way you feel. My home don't feel like home, Shavi. I'm gon' let you make it, though, because this is partially my fault. But, I'm gon' give you this shit so good, yo' ass gon' be ruined for anybody else."

Oh, thank God. He didn't know who I'd slept with. He grabbed my neck and lightly choked me as he leaned over me and fucked me hard. "You hear me? Don't give my shit to nobody else or I'm gon' fuck you up, next time."

I released a moan. "I'm sorry, Daddy."

❦ 16 ❦

O mari

"Did his dick touch your soul like mine, Shavi?"

"Noooo," she moaned.

I couldn't believe she admitted that she'd slept with someone else. My pride was a lil hurt, but I couldn't say shit about it. We'd been apart for almost two weeks and I'd slept with Mali last weekend. She'd brought her lil thick ass over here, late one night. We'd fucked around for at least two hours. She still couldn't take the dick like Ashahve, but whatever. I felt bad after the fact, but I didn't now. My attempt to bluff her had bit me in the ass. I couldn't feel shit different about her pussy.

Continuing to fuck her hard was bringing my nut to the surface fast, but I was trying to hurt her. I wanted her to be out of commission for a couple of days. Women usually didn't move on that fast from hurt, at least not the ones I dealt with. Ashahve was like a damn nigga, thinking with her pussy. *What the fuck?* That shit kind of fucked my head up, for real. It didn't fuck it up enough for a nigga to go soft, but it made me angry. All I could visualize was another nigga hitting this shit from the back, like I was.

I pulled her head back by her hair and thrusted harder than I ever had. Most women couldn't take it, so I never got a chance to kill it like this. "Omariiii... shit!" she whispered.

"Take this dick, Shavi. Take all this shit. I bet you'll think twice about fucking another nigga."

I couldn't have her imagining or thinking about another nigga while she was with me. There was no way I could think about Mali's ass when I was in Ashahve's pussy. This shit was diamond encrusted. Her love for me was deep, and I knew that. I guess like mine, her body had needs. When Mali had called, I was all in my fucking feelings about Shavi not answering my phone calls or text messages. I'd never had a female ignore me like that.

Normally, I would have said fuck her and moved the fuck on. But this shit between her legs and that shit in her chest had a nigga sprung as fuck. Her heart was so damn big. So, I told Mali to come get her insides fucked up and she'd gotten here within five minutes of our conversation, like she was driving by my shit, just in case I said yes. She'd sucked my dick like her life depended on it and told me how much she missed it. Then, before she left, her exact words were, *I guess your lil girlfriend ain't fucking you right.*

I cussed her ass out, then told her if she ever mentioned Shavi again, I'd choke the fuck out of her. How the fuck she even knew who Ashahve was had put me on high alert. They didn't run in the same circles, but she'd called her by name. When she'd left, I'd beat myself up for fucking her and put all my energy into trying to get Ashahve to talk to me, not knowing she was getting her pussy stroked.

My dick had enlarged itself inside of Shavi, and I knew I was about to fire off. "Fuuuuck... this pussy finna drain my dick, shawty. Where you want this shit?" Before she could answer, I answered my own damn question. "Naw, never mind. I want this shit all over your face."

I pulled out of her and quickly rolled her over and shot my seed in her face. Her face was scrunched up. I'd never done that to her before, so I didn't know what she was gonna say. Quickly getting off her to get a towel, I came back to find her in the same position, with her eyes squeezed tightly. After gently wiping her face clean, I went back to the bathroom to rinse the towel. She was completely quiet, not saying a word and I didn't know how to take that.

After cleaning my dick off, I went back to the room to find her sitting on the bed with tears streaming down her cheeks. I felt bad as shit. I'd let my anger and jealousy control me. I handed her the towel and she stood from the bed and went to the bathroom. When she did, I saw a little blood on my sheets. Damn, she must have started her period.

I pulled the sheets off the bed, then got dressed, so I could put them in the washer. Before I could leave the room, Shavi had exited the bathroom. I dropped the sheets on the floor, then walked over to her and pulled her close. "I'm sorry. I lost my shit a lil bit."

"It's okay. I deserved that. I have to go home and soak. My shit gon' be sore if I don't. My stomach is already cramping."

"Yeah, there was blood on the sheets. You started your cycle?"

"I guess. It's getting close to that time. There was blood there when I wiped."

"Aight. I'll wash the towel with these sheets. You okay?"

"Yeah. I'm sorry, Omari. I was vulnerable. That shouldn't have happened."

"It's aight. Let's just go from here."

Her apologizing to me was making me feel worse about being hard on her for doing the same shit I had done. I pulled her in my arms and hugged her tightly. When I released her, she was walking funny. Shaking my head slowly as I dropped it, I walked over to her to help her. "Shavi, maybe you should soak here, so yo' mama don't try to find out what happened."

She smirked at me. "You're probably right."

I smiled at her, then left her side to go run water in the tub... a degree beneath boiling. Women could stand that hot ass water and I couldn't understand how. That water felt like somebody was throwing fire darts at my ass the last time I tried to slip in the shower with Shavi. When I came out, she was still standing in the same spot. I led her to the tub and helped her undress again. Damn, I'd lost control and nearly killed her ass.

❦

"Da-dy?"

"Good morning, princess! Happy birthday!" I said, excitedly, as I entered Jordynn's room.

I was heading to her room to see if she wanted her Eggo Pancakes this morning. She had sat up in the bed and was trying to get out. "Thank you, Da-dy."

"You're welcome, baby girl."

I helped her to the bathroom, although she liked swinging on the crutches. "Da-dy, is Shavi still here?"

"No, she left about an hour ago. She's coming back, though. Guess who else is coming over for your birthday?"

"Mommy?"

I had to control myself, because I almost rolled my eyes and cursed. Piper was her mother and she loved her. In Jordynn's eyes, Piper had done nothing wrong. Remembering that was the hard part. Piper was still in the hospital. Her mama had called, earlier yesterday, before Shavi had gotten here, to tell me that they were finally moving her to a regular room. That wreck had fucked her up something serious. I was at the point, now, that I didn't care whether she did time anymore. The way her body was all fucked up was punishment enough.

She'd had a few broken ribs, one of which had punctured a lung, swelling on her brain and multiple broken bones throughout her body, including in her face. So, she was gonna be in pain for a long time. Right now, she still couldn't talk or walk, and she was desperately trying to tell her mama something about what had happened. "Naw, shawty. Na-na and Papa."

Her eyes brightened. "Yay!"

I smiled at her as my phone alerted me that I'd received a text message. After helping baby girl to the couch, so she could eat, I grabbed the phone from the countertop. It was Mali. *What the fuck did she want?* When I opened the message, I almost shit a brick. That sneaky bitch had taken pictures of us fucking. We'd been in a position where she had straddled my lap in a sitting position, and she'd taken a selfie while we were fucking. Although my face wasn't on the screen, my tattoos would definitely identify me. Another one came through of me hitting her from the back. My face was visible in that one.

It took everything in me not to call and go off on her ass. Then, I thought about it. Why was she sending me these pictures? Before I could panic about the unknown, she enlightened me. *Your precious Ashahve got these pictures, too. Thanks to your clock in the corner of the picture, she'll know exactly when this happened.*

I was pacing in my kitchen, nervous as fuck. My clock illuminated the date as well, so I couldn't even lie about when it happened. *What in the fuck was I gonna do?* How in the hell did she get Shavi's phone number? I bet her ass was the same mutha-fucka that sent those pictures to Ashahve of that lady holding my hand at my job. Sweat had begun to accumulate on my brow. I sent her a text. *You triflin' ass bitch.*

She sent back the laughing emojis and I wanted to throw my damn phone. "Da-dy? What's wrong?"

I broke from the trance I was in and smiled at my baby girl. "Nothing, baby. Daddy's okay."

She went back to her cartoons as I placed the frozen pancakes in the toaster. Shortly after, Shavi forwarded the same pictures to me. I didn't know what to say. She sent another text. *So, looks like you were getting your dick wet while we were apart. I see I wasn't the only one that couldn't hold out. However, I was the only one that got made to feel like I was a hoe. Who is this bitch?*

I wiped my hand down my face and kept my eyes closed for a minute. Looking back at my phone, I tried to offer an explanation. *I'm sorry, Shavi. It wasn't my intent to make you feel like a hoe. You're far from that. Her name is Mali. I'm not sure how she got your number or how she even knows who you are. I think she's the same one that probably sent the pic of me at work.*

Jordynn's pancakes popped up from the toaster, so I put them on a plate and drizzled syrup over them, then brought them to her with a small glass of orange juice. "Thank you, Da-dy."

"You're welcome, birthday girl."

I went back to the kitchen and put the rest of the pancakes in the freezer. Shavi still hadn't responded and that shit had me on edge. Anxiety was crippling me. I wanted Shavi and me to work out. She was who was out here for me. I knew that, without a shadow of a doubt, but what I didn't know was why I kept fucking up. As I leaned against the countertop, my eyes closed involuntarily.

Shavi was supposed to be picking up everything for me. Hopefully, that would still happen. She was supposed to be getting the cake, ice cream and balloons. I expelled those thoughts from my mind. Letting Jordynn down would be the last thing she would do, even if Jordynn's dad was an asshole. I didn't even know why I'd tried to bluff her. The idea of her sleeping with someone while we were apart was her business. I shouldn't have brought that shit up.

Once Jordynn finished breakfast, I gave her medicine and laid her back in the bed. She almost went straight to sleep. I'd cleaned the house yesterday, so the only thing I had to do was prepare the hotdogs and French fries when everyone arrived. Piper's mother said she would come, too, since Piper was now in a regular room. Also, Piper's aunt was going to stay up there while Ms. Joyce came here.

After I made my bed, I laid across it, attempting to take a nap, but my phone chimed. It was that stupid bitch. *For good measure, I sent her a couple more. One of them shows just how much you were enjoying my pussy.*

She sent the pics to me, and my head was dropped back, and my eyes were closed. I remembered that exact moment. It was then that I'd started thinking about Shavi and had bust not long after. I didn't know why Mali was suddenly so interested in destroying my relationship. She'd never acted like she wanted to be more than what we were. She was never a prospect to me. We'd agreed that we would fuck and that would be the extent of it.

So, I couldn't understand why she was going out of her way to make me miserable. After we'd fucked in the shower, that one time, when I'd damn near crippled her ass, she didn't call me for months. This shit was puzzling and confusing as hell. Maybe, in the beginning, the bitch was just missing the shit I put down on her and wanted to assure that I wouldn't hold out on her ass. Her reason for the bullshit she'd done today was probably some sick shit she was doing because I dissed her ass before she left.

Trying to figure out this shit was stressing me the fuck out. I decided to just let it go and try to mend things with Shavi. I knew she was pissed. What I'd done to her last night, because I was in my feelings, probably humiliated her and she accepted it as punishment for what she'd done. I allowed her to feel like shit about what she'd done all while the skeletons in my closet were having a damn party.

An hour later, there was a knock at the door. I peeled myself from the bed, went to the door and opened it to find Ashahve and Mr. and Mrs. Glasper. Shavi had a scowl on her face, when she looked at me, and I couldn't blame her. Mrs. Glasper smiled brightly and opened her arms to embrace me. After hugging her and shaking Mr. Glasper's hand, I invited them in and let them know Jordynn was asleep. They made themselves comfortable on my sofa... the same sofa I'd fucked Shavi on numerous times. I joined Shavi in the kitchen as she pulled paper plates, napkins and plastic spoons from the bag. Taking the ice cream from the countertop, I put it in the freezer and sat the quarter sheet cake of Disney princesses on the table.

I went back to the kitchen area and started boiling water for the wieners and poured oil in another pot for the French fries. Shavi was about to walk off, so I grabbed her arm. She turned and slapped the shit out of me. That shit practically made me snap. I yanked her from her feet and roughly sat her on the countertop. She winced, then frowned deeply. "Look, Shavi. I'm sorry. I fucked up, yet again."

"Omari, you're a fucking asshole. But you know... I'm petty as hell, and I can fuck you up in ways you wouldn't imagine. You've never seen this side of me, and I never wanted you to see it, but I want you to hurt. The way you treated me last night was fucked up, and I accepted that shit because I felt bad about sleeping with someone else. Now, I just wanna punch you until I get tired. How the fuck you gon' make me feel bad about doing the same thing you did? That was some cold shit. You were just gonna allow me to think you were pining after me, the whole time."

She shook her head slowly, as her upper lip twitched. "I said I'm sorry, Shavi. Honestly, I never expected you to admit the shit. I didn't think you had slept with anyone else. I was fucking wit'chu. But when you apologized for doing what I was accusing you of, it set me the fuck off. Even though I'd done it, I never expected you to do it, too. I love the fuck outta you. Real shit."

She hopped off the counter and walked down the hallway to Jordynn's bedroom and closed the door. Before I could head back there, with her, someone knocked at the front door. I went to it to find Ms. Joyce.

"Hey, Rich. How are you, baby?"

"I'm okay, Ms. Joyce. Come on in."

I stepped aside, letting her inside, then closed the door. After introducing Ms. Joyce to the Glaspers, I finished preparing the hotdogs and prayed that Ashahve would forgive me. Jordynn's birthday was supposed to be a joyous occasion. If Ashahve couldn't move past this, I didn't know what I would do. My actions had fucked her in her ass, without a lubricant. I hurt her and, somehow, I would have to be so good to her, that she forgot about it.

17

E lijah

"I've been seeing Ashahve Glasper. I know you said that I shouldn't, but I can't say no to her. I didn't initiate the contact, but once the contact was made, I couldn't say no to it."

"Elijah, this isn't good for you. Your love for this woman is too potent. You can't expect to get better, especially if she decides to leave you again."

"She won't completely cut me off. I understand the risk I'm taking. However, I've been taking my medicine religiously, not skipping a single dosage. We have an understanding and I've accepted it. Had I been more open with her in the beginning, we'd be a couple."

She sighed loudly and dropped her head to her hand. "Elijah, you are so stubborn. You cannot live in the past. I hate when you say if you would've done this or that. It's in the past and there's nothing you can do to change it. All you can do now is make wise decisions.

Seeing Ashahve is not a wise decision. However, I can only offer my advice. I can't make you accept it."

Dr. Madison was making me feel like a disobedient child. It was like she was saying, *I done told you, but I'm gon' let you fall on your face.* I knew she was probably right, but Ashahve Glasper was my addiction. My need for her was so great that, some days, I couldn't function until I'd heard from her. It had been a week since we'd had sex. We'd only talked on the phone, once, since then, but I texted her at least once a day. I couldn't help it.

I nodded my head, in acceptance of what she had to say. "Well, our hour is up, Elijah. I'll see you next week."

She was angry with me for the decision I was making. Most times, she'd walk me out and we'd laugh and talk a little before I left. I saw her usually once every other week, but since I started talking to Ashahve again, I started coming once a week. The decision I'd made to talk to her again, and lastly to have sex with her, would come at a cost if I didn't stay in the right frame of mind. I knew Ashahve cared for me, but I also knew she was using me. Even with knowledge of that fact, I still wanted to be near her.

When I left, I decided to head to Karen's house. My little sister had said she would cook today and invited me over. Karen was a chef, so her cooking skills were impeccable. That being said, she rarely cooked at home, because she cooked all day. Since it was just her, she would often bring dinner home from whatever she'd cooked at her restaurant that day. She used to always say she wanted to be like Emeril Lagasse and G. Garvin. I'd never seen a kid that watched cooking shows, all the time, like Karen.

I used to laugh at her and she would roll her eyes and tell me to find some business. I was extremely proud of her, though, for following her dreams. Following her dreams occasionally allowed me to eat like the elite of Beaumont, Texas. I could practically taste those roasted short ribs with carrots and mushrooms. Sis was the real deal. I'd told her, once, that she'd surpassed Mama's cooking skills, but I'd kill her if she ever told Mama I said that.

I got out of the car and headed to her door. Before I could ring the doorbell, she'd opened it. "Eli! Hey!"

"Hey, sis! You look great!"

"So do you! I hear congratulations are in order."

I frowned slightly, trying to figure out what she was talking about. After closing the door, she said, "Mama told me you'll be teaching a graduate course!"

"Yeah! I'm excited about that."

I was excited alright, for all the wrong reasons. As I followed her in the kitchen, my phone chimed, alerting me of a text message. *Hi, Elijah. Can I come over later?*

Hmm. That was interesting. Ashahve wanted to come over. She'd told me that we probably wouldn't be seeing each other again, the same way we did last weekend. I thought she would avoid seeing me, period. I replied, *Sure. I'll let you know when I get home.*

Okay.

"Everything okay?"

"Oh, yeah. Just responding to a colleague. Do you need any help in here?"

"Nope. Go have a seat at the table. I just have to fix our plates."

I lifted my hands in surrender. "You got it."

She was a maniac when it came to people being in her kitchen. Especially while she was "creating," as she would say. I would always ask her, *When did cooking become creating?* She'd laugh and say *I'm creating a dish that will knock your taste buds out'cha mouth. Now, back up!* I would ultimately end up doing whatever she told me to do. While I was the oldest, she had always been the boss.

I sat at the table where she'd set a glass of water and had a bottle of wine in a bucket of ice. After taking a sip of the water, my phone started ringing. When I saw Ashahve's name on the screen, I got nervous. She rarely ever called. "Hello?"

"Hi, Elijah."

I could hear the sadness in her tone, and my heart became mush. Standing from my seat, I went out to Karen's patio. "Hey. You okay?"

"I guess. I'm on my way to Omari's to celebrate his daughter's birthday. But I just got two picture messages of him fucking somebody else."

My mushy heart hardened with every word she said. After a moment of quietness and me gathering my thoughts, I said, "Well, you slept with me. He just doesn't have pictures of it."

"I know, but that's not what bothers me."

"Then what is?"

"He treated me horribly last night, because he sensed that I'd slept with someone else. I admitted that I had. What's blowing me is that he treated me that way, knowing he'd done the same thing. What the fuck?"

"I'm sorry, baby. Just try to calm down and count down the hours until you're with me. I'll make it better for you. Holding you in my arms soothes my soul, so I can only hope that it soothes yours as well."

"Thank you, Elijah. I'll see you later."

"Okay. I'll message you when I leave my sister's house."

"Okay."

I went back inside to find Karen bringing our plates to the table. Quickly voiding my face of the emotions I was feeling, I smiled and sniffed dramatically. "That looks and smells delicious."

"Oh, it is. You about to find out."

"So damn cocky."

"I learned from the best."

I rolled my eyes. When it came to our jobs, we were both cocky. We knew we were amazing at what we did and didn't allow anyone else to tell us otherwise. "Yes, you did. Nobody can touch your skills, sis."

"You right, and nobody can touch you in a classroom."

We both sat at the table and I stretched my arms across the table. Karen put her hands in mine, and I said grace. My mind went to Ashahve, at that moment, but I quickly pushed her to the back of it, for now. The second those ribs touched my tongue, I was in food euphoria. "Damn, Karen. This is amazing."

"Thank you."

She beamed with pride as we sat and ate, making light conversation. In the quiet moments, I couldn't help but think of Ashahve.

As I headed home, for the evening, and was about to message Shavi to let her know, my phone rang. I was thinking that she was calling me before I could call her, but I was surprised to see the call was coming from Nyera. We didn't talk as often but, occasionally, she'd call to see how I was doing. "Hello?"

"Hi, Elijah. How are you?"

"Hey, Nyera. I'm good. How are you?"

"I'm okay. Are you ready for school to start? We only have two more weeks."

"I know, but I'm ready. Summer is always slow for me, since I rarely go anywhere."

"Why don't you?"

"I don't know. Last summer I went to Paris, but it's not the same when you go places alone. So, if I'm gonna be lonely, I might as well be lonely at home."

"I suppose I can understand that. Are you busy tomorrow?"

"Umm... no. What's up?"

"You wanna go to brunch at Suga's?"

"Sure. What time?"

"How about ten or eleven?"

"That sounds good. I'll pick you up."

This whole conversation seemed kind of awkward, but I guess that was because I would be seeing Ashahve later. They seemed to have a good relationship and I'd hate to come between them. It wasn't like Ashahve and I didn't have something before Nyera came along, but maybe we should have been upfront with her about it, in the beginning when we'd seen one another at Floyd's that night. It wasn't like Nyera and I were together anymore.

"So, umm... I'm nervous."

"What are you nervous about?"

"It will be my first semester teaching here, well, teaching college. I don't know what to expect."

"I promise you that you will do fine. It's not like high school. You pretty much do what you want and teach how you want to teach. Most of the people in those classes are there because they want to be. You don't have to worry about disruptions and whether you turned in your lesson plans. You're going to love it."

She took a deep breath and I could hear the nervousness when she exhaled. "I'm gonna need a few mimosas tomorrow."

I chuckled, then texted Ashahve to tell her I was home. "Well, Nyera, I have to go. I just got home, and I have to carry in some food my sister cooked for me."

"Okay. Well, I'll talk to you in the morning."

"Okay. Bye."

I got out of my car and grabbed my to-go bag Karen had packed me. Ashahve was the person on my mind when I'd asked for it. I was so full, I probably wouldn't eat anything else for the rest of the day. Heading inside, I went straight to the shower, so whenever she got here, I would be ready for whatever she had in mind.

18

A shahve

"CAN WE TALK?"

Omari had whispered in my ear, right before we were about to leave. I didn't have time for his bullshit. Last night had been horrible. I thought my period had started, but I was wrong. He'd fucked me so hard, I bled. When he shot his nut in my face, without asking me if that was okay, I felt so damn low. I'd accepted his reaction to my admission, though.

But now, to know that he'd fucked someone else and I had to see the proof, had infuriated me. How in the fuck was he gonna tell me what I shouldn't have done if he had done the same? I wasn't upset that he'd fucked that chick. I was upset that he treated me like his hoe. When I got home last night, and didn't see a drop of blood in my underwear, I knew he'd caused the bleeding. The way he fucked me was something I'd never experienced before. When I got home, I looked up what could have caused me to bleed. Realizing that the rough sex could have broken a blood vessel in my cervix, I knew I was probably okay.

My period wasn't due for another week and a half, so I was good there, too. What I endured last night, with Omari, was embarrassing and heart breaking. Then, to find out that he was only bluffing me, made me angrier. I followed him to the bedroom, as my lip twitched, leaving my parents in the front room with Jordynn and her grand-mother. When he closed the door, he turned to me and said, "I'm really sorry, Ashahve."

"Your apology means nothing to me, right now. This shit is so overwhelming, I don't even know what to think."

"I want to make this right. I've already apologized so much until I've lost count. I'm willing to do whatever to make it right."

"I don't know if I want you to! How do I know you won't do more fucked up shit? Now I see the bullshit Piper probably went through with your ass!"

He lowered his head and it looked like he got mad for a second. I didn't give a fuck that he was angry. Now he knew how I felt. "Who was it?"

"Who was who?"

"Who you had sex with?"

"Why are you worried about that? Had your bitch not texted me, I wouldn't know about you having sex with anybody."

"Man, Shavi, quit playing! Who was it?"

"I'm not playing. Why can't you just leave me alone, especially now, while I'm angry?"

"Yeah. I wouldn't be surprised if you slept with your professor."

My head tilted sideways. He just wanted to go there with me. I was boiling on the inside and this shit was about to bubble over on his ass. "You know what, Omari? I sure did. And the dick was amazing."

What I saw in his eyes scared the hell out of me. As I was about to walk away, he grabbed me by the neck and backed me against the wall. I could barely breathe. He had to have lost his mind, as I scratched his hand, trying to get him to loosen his hold on me. The tears fell from my eyes as he finally released me. It was like he snapped. I stormed off to his bathroom as I coughed. "Fuck! Why would you say some shit like that, Shavi? Maybe you right. This whole shit done escalated and I ain't tryna catch a case with you. Just leave."

After I composed myself, I walked back into his room and looked in his eyes. "Fuck you."

I flung the door open, as he stood there with anger in his eyes. Walking down the hall, I felt like I wanted to crumble. I never saw things going this way with Omari. I loved him so much, and that was the shit that was hurting me the most. I'd given him my heart, only for him to break it. "Ashahve," he called out.

Even as angry as I was, the tenderness in his voice halted my progress. I stood frozen in place, in the hallway, as I felt him approach me from behind. "I love you. I know I've had a fucked-up way of showing it lately, but I do."

I turned to him, as the tears threatened to fall from my eyes. When I looked in his eyes, I could see the emotion about to spill from them. Omari rarely showed his emotions and seeing him that way only made the tears fall from my eyes. He reached out to me and grabbed my hand. "I'm sorry for everything."

He gently wiped the tears that had fallen down my cheeks. I nodded, then turned to leave. Taking a deep breath, I walked around the corner and plastered a smile on my face. "Mama, Daddy, are y'all ready?"

They both stood from their seats and gave Jordynn love. She looked so sad that we were leaving. I sat next to her and hugged her tightly. "I love you, baby cakes."

I kissed her cheek as she said, "I love you, Shavi. Are you coming over tomorrow?"

"No, baby. I have to work."

That was the easiest explanation of why I wouldn't be coming over, tomorrow. But I wouldn't be coming over ever again.

"EVERYTHING'S GONNA BE OKAY. You'll see."

I was lying in Elijah's arms, crying my eyes out. I'd dropped my parents at home and came straight here. Before going to Omari's, I'd asked him if it was okay if I came over tonight and he'd said yes. I'd called Tia to see if she wanted to go out, but she was at work. I was becoming more and more skeptical about what was going on with her. She never had time for me these days. She'd already graduated and had taken the summer to just work. She usually went to school during the summer sessions. Once she'd declined to go out, I messaged Elijah. As always, he was there for me and said he would message me when he got home.

I didn't know that the situation with Omari would get worse, so I had even more to tell him. Hopefully Omari didn't confront him about us sleeping together. I'd never intended to tell him, but he had pushed me and, before I could stop it, my mouth spit some real fly shit at him and almost got me fucked up. I still couldn't believe he'd choked me.

Elijah had messaged me right as we were leaving Omari's to tell me he was home. So, after dropping my parents off, I came straight here. He'd immediately pulled me in his arms and held me to his chest. I hugged him around his waist and accepted the consolation his embrace brought me. We were now on the couch, and I'd told him what had happened today. When I told him that I'd told Omari that I'd slept with him, his eyebrows had risen.

"I hope you're right, Elijah. Omari needs counseling, I think. He has so many issues he needs to deal with, mainly the death of his mother. In the meantime, I can't be there. The line was crossed last night with the way he handled me, but today was an even bigger sign that I needed to let go. When he grabbed me by the neck, it scared the shit out of me. How far would he have gone if we would have been alone?"

"I'm so sorry you had to go through that. I know what it's like, though, to see red. Even though he coaxed you, pushed you to tell him who you'd slept with, you probably should have just walked away. Knowing that you'd come back to me was too much for him."

I took a deep breath and snuggled closer to him as he rubbed my head, then kissed it. We remained quiet for a while. Between my legs was still sore and it was starting to throb a little. I shifted on the couch and looked up at Elijah. He smiled softly, then kissed my lips. I kissed him back softly, allowing my body to relax even more, as his hands traveled to my ass, pulling me to his lap. I tried to straddle him, but I winced in pain and Elijah noticed.

I hadn't told him how roughly Omari had fucked me last night. I hadn't told him that we had sex at all. "What's the matter, Shavi?"

"Nothing."

I stood and sat next to him again. He didn't push. He probably just figured I didn't want to be in a position to have sex with him. Again, I snuggled into him and fell asleep.

When I awakened, I could smell food and my stomach growled. I didn't eat hotdogs at Omari's because I was so pissed. Being as angry as I was had stolen my appetite. Sitting up, I slid on my flip flops and went to the kitchen, to find Elijah heating up food. "Hey. How did you sleep?"

"I slept okay. Thank you."

"So, you have one semester of school left until you get your bachelor's degree. Are you gonna jump right into graduate school, or are you going to wait until next fall?"

"I'm jumping right in. There's no point in stalling. I am going to apply to teach Sociology at BISD, though, since I'll have my teaching certification, too. That way, I can get away from Bath and Body Works."

He smiled as if he were reminiscing, then said, "That sounds great. Well, guess who will be teaching a graduate course?"

My eyebrows lifted. "Wow! Congratulations!"

He chuckled. "Thank you, Shavi. So, it looks like our tenure isn't done yet. Depending on how well this class goes, they may add another by next semester."

I could tell that he was extremely proud of his accomplishments and I was happy for him, too. "That's awesome! I'm so happy and excited for you."

He blushed, then turned away to get a pan from the oven. "Thank you."

"What is that? It smells so good."

As if on cue, my stomach growled loudly. It seemed I was always hungry when I came here. Elijah chuckled and I did, too. There was no need in being embarrassed anymore. He probably expected that to happen when I came over. "My sister cooked for me today and sent some home with me. It's roasted short ribs with carrots and mushrooms, along with mashed potatoes and green beans."

"She's a chef, right?"

"Yep. Her cooking skills amaze me."

I took out two glasses and Elijah said, "I'm not eating, Shavi. I'm still full, from earlier. I mainly brought this home for you."

"How sweet. Thank you."

"You know you always starving. I gotta make sure you keep your strength up."

I playfully slapped his arm. "Whatever."

He laughed as I poured some tea, then brought my plate to the table. I sniffed dramatically and said, "My God. I'm gonna have to thank your sister myself."

He rolled his eyes, then said, "Nyera called me today."

I broke my gaze away from the food and looked at him. Nyera had been somewhat distant since we had the conversation about Omari. I thought it was just because she and Elijah weren't together anymore. "That's cool. Is she wanting you back?"

"I don't think so. I think she just wants to maintain a friendship. She asked for me to go with her to brunch tomorrow. Other than that, our short conversation was about school starting."

When he said that, I realized Jordynn would be starting her first day of pre-k on Monday. I had to be there for that. Maybe Omari and I could put our differences aside to see her off. As if I'd summoned him, my phone chimed, with his personalized tune, alerting me of a text. Taking it from my pocket, I unlocked the screen as Elijah watched me.

How did we get here? I can't believe I let the woman I love slip through my grasp. I'm so sorry for putting my hands on you, Shavi. I just saw red when you said what you said. I can't even bear to type it. The way things have been going for the past couple of weeks have been crazy. I do feel that we were meant to be, but maybe we had the wrong timing. Maybe I was supposed to go through all this bullshit alone, so I could be better for you when it was done. I don't know. But what I do know is that I love you. I always will. I hope you can forgive me.

The tears were free-falling again. I laid my phone, face-down, on the table without responding. Falling into an abusive relationship wasn't on my to-do list and it seemed that's where things between me and Omari were going. More often than not, I wondered if we moved too fast. Elijah came and sat next to me and put his arm around me. "He's human, Shavi. If he realizes he needs help, that's a good thing. Does he realize it?"

"Yes."

"Then don't shut him out. We won't have any more than what we have right now. It would hurt your cousin and your family if we did. So, more than anything else, I want you to be happy. While I would want to be the one to make you happy, I saw how happy he makes you. You're angry and hurt. I get that. But once things have calmed down, the two of you need to talk."

I looked up at him and kissed his lips, then looked back down at my food. He chuckled and shook his head. "Finish eating."

"Thank you, Elijah, for being an amazing friend. I'm not sure what's going on with Tia. She never wants to hang anymore, and she rarely even has time to text, let alone talk. I've been racking my brain, trying to think if maybe I did or said something to offend her, but I keep coming up empty."

"One thing I've learned in my life is that people you think are for you, and your biggest cheerleaders, can sometimes be your worst enemy. The worst enemy is the one you don't see coming. I can deal with an enemy I know about. It's the ones that are pretending to love you that are the most dangerous. You trust them with your life, thinking they have your best interest at heart, not knowing that they are praying for your downfall."

I thought about what he said. Surely, Tia wasn't against me. But that was the only logical explanation. We used to talk about everything, but lately, like for the past year, I'd been the only one talking. Instead of dwelling on it, I finished off my ribs, then brought my dishes to the sink. "Ashahve, since when do I allow you to clean your dishes here? You know I'll take care of it."

I stared up at him and I saw his body tremble. He walked over to me and stood behind me as I rinsed out my plate to put it in the dishwasher. My body heated up as he wrapped his arms around my waist. I felt his erection, but I knew there was no way I could handle sex after Omari left his mark. He said he would ruin me, and I believed he did. The problem was that he ruined me for him, too. Although I was somewhat turned on, I wasn't nearly as turned on as I normally would be.

When Omari fucked me, toward the end, I started to dry out because he was hurting me. It wasn't pleasurable anymore. I didn't even think he noticed. "Hey. You okay?"

I didn't realize it until Elijah's interruption, but I was whimpering, as the tears slid down my cheeks. Elijah turned me to him. "What's going on, Shavi? You've been zoning out quite a bit."

I lowered my head, resting my forehead against his shoulder blade. He lifted my head, holding it steady by placing his fingertips underneath my chin, forcing me to look into his eyes. "Omari was really umm... rough with me last night. When he said he knew I'd had sex with someone else, it was while we were having sex. When I admitted I had, he got rough. So rough until I started bleeding. I'm really sore down there. I never wanna say that I know what a rape victim feels like, but I can probably imagine now."

Elijah had turned extremely red. I didn't want to tell him but, with the way I was spacing out, I couldn't keep it a secret any longer. "Listen, Elijah. It's okay. I'm just sore, that's all. I looked it up and it's very common for women to bleed after rough sex. I'm okay. I just keep thinking about it."

I rested my hands on his cheeks, trying to bring him back from wherever he went, internally. It seemed to work, because he leaned over and kissed my lips. "Come on. Let me take care of you."

Elijah brought me to his room and laid me in the bed, then went to his bathroom. He started the water running in his air tub as I laid there staring at the ceiling. I didn't know what he'd put in the water, but it smelled soothing. When he came back in the room, he helped me from the bed. "What did you put in the water?"

"A lavender pain relief body soak by Dr. Teals. I got it from Walmart when my muscles were aching."

"Epsom salt?"

"Yeah."

"Okay."

Once we were in the bathroom, he helped me disrobe, occasionally kissing my skin in various places, as my body relaxed in the wanting it felt for him. He grabbed my hand and I lifted my leg to get inside. When I slid down in the tub, I cringed, then almost immediately relaxed, letting out a sigh. "I'm gonna let you relax, and I'll check in on you in a few."

"Thank you."

He nodded his head, then turned on some smooth sounds by The Internet and left the room. I slid in the tub, a little further, and rested my head on the small pillow he'd put there. Letting the smooth sounds permeate my very being, I did what Elijah said to do. I relaxed.

✿ 19 ✿

O mari

CAN I come with you for Jordynn's first day tomorrow?

I was so excited to receive a text from Ashahve. Yesterday, I was so depressed after she left. I'd allowed a few tears to escape, just thinking about how badly I'd hurt her... how I pushed her away. Today, Jordynn and I went to the cemetery to sit at my mama's grave. I'd brought her headphones and a tablet so she could watch YouTube while I talked to my mama about how I'd made a mess of things. I thought I loved Piper, years ago, but, after being with Ashahve, I knew she was my first love. The hurt I felt when Piper fucked me over was nothing in comparison to how I felt now.

I messaged Ashahve back. *Of course. We will leave the apartment about seven.*

She'd never responded to my text last night, so I thought she was done with me for good. I wasn't gonna get my hopes up about being a couple again, but just to know that she loved Jordynn so much until she was willing to be around me just to see her, made my heart light. It was why I fell in love with her. She had a beautiful heart. Jordynn and I had been in the house for a couple of hours and I think she could tell that I was depressed. She kind of stayed away from me.

As I laid on the sofa, hoping Ashahve would text me again, just to say anything, my phone started ringing indicating I had someone who wanted to facetime. When I picked it up from the coffee table and saw Piper's name, my eyebrows lifted, and I quickly answered. When she saw my face, she started crying. I damn near wanted to cry, looking at her face. It was still swollen around her nose and I noticed her mouth was wired shut. She had a few tubes still on her. Ms. Joyce took the phone. "Hey, Rich. When she calms down a little bit, she wants to talk to you, then Jordynn. I told her she should wait until she was a little better, but she wouldn't hear of it."

"Hey, Ms. Joyce. When did she start talking?"

"This morning. You'll have to listen carefully, because her speech is a little slurred, plus with her mouth wired shut, it makes it that much more difficult to understand her."

I nodded as she handed the phone back to Piper. "Hi, Rich."

"Hey, Piper."

"Please, just listen." She took a few breaths. "When I left Jordynn with you, I thought that you would see how hard it was being a single parent and that you would want to be with the mother of your child. I don't know what the hell I was thinking. Jordynn is your everything and I should've known you would man up and take care of her."

She started crying again. "I never wanted to hurt Tutu. That's my baby. I love her so much. When I came back, I was so broken and embarrassed. I knew you would be angry, but I never thought you would be as protective of Jordynn as you were. It made me angry that you were treating me like I would do something to Jordynn. Like I was a monster or something. I decided since you wanted to be like that, I would play your game until you let your guard down."

Ms. Joyce wiped her tears. Her other arm was in a cast, up to her shoulder, so she couldn't raise it to do that herself. She continued.

"Then, you finally did. I wanted to hit you where it hurt. I know you love Jordynn with everything in you. So, I decided that I would take her. I'm sorry, Rich. I was playing games, because I wanted you back. After you fell for Shavi, I knew I would have to do something drastic to get your attention. That shit didn't work."

She broke down as I stared at her. I hadn't said a word, the whole time she was talking. I wanted to just listen, like she told me to do. Although I still didn't understand her reasoning and the way she did things, I said, "I forgive you, Piper. You're suffering enough. I just want to co-parent with the Piper from a year ago. The Piper that was on her grown woman shit. Jordynn loves you and she seems unaffected by what you did. She was more affected by how I responded to what you did. She wanted to be with her mama. So, I'm sorry, too, Piper. I'm sorry for pushing you away when my mama died, too. I know I was difficult to deal with."

She cried even more. I'd never apologized to her for anything. My whole life, I'd been an asshole to people. While being a father had matured me in some areas, it hadn't matured me in every area. I was inconsiderate of people's feelings, just letting my mouth fire off whatever the fuck it wanted to. Piper went through hell with me and I didn't realize that shit until she took Jordynn. The way I treated Ashahve was embarrassing. "Rich?"

"Yeah?"

"Thank you for that."

"You're welcome, Piper."

"The guy that was in the car was just catching a ride with us. I knew him from when I was working at Kroger, years ago. He worked there, too. Me and Tutu had stopped at McDonald's to get something to eat and he was in there. He asked if I could bring him a couple of miles up the road and I agreed. Before we got in the wreck, he was tryna light up in my car. We were arguing because he wanted to smoke weed in front of Tutu. So, I told him he could get his ass out and walk. Because I was so busy arguing with him, I missed the stop sign."

She took a few deep breaths, then Ms. Joyce put a straw in her mouth for her to sip some water. Talking to her was hard. It was hard because it was like looking in a mirror. I saw all the wrong I'd done to her and Ashahve. Lowering my head, I played with the drawstring on my shorts. I looked back at the screen to see Piper looking at me. "I'll bring Jordynn to see you, next weekend, if you're still there. Jordynn thought he was your boyfriend. Why did that nigga leave y'all, not knowing if y'all were okay or not?"

She shook her head. "Because he's a selfish, inconsiderate, cold, son of a bitch. He had a warrant and didn't wanna go to jail. That was all I remembered him saying. I passed out while listening to my baby screaming. It was my fault and my baby got hurt. She kept screaming for me to help her and I couldn't do a thing. She was in so much pain and it killed me that I'd put her in harm's way. The police found his ass and arrested him, but that shit ain't gon' reverse what happened."

I stood from the sofa and went to Jordynn's room. When I got to her doorway, she said, "Hey, Da-dy."

"Hi, baby. I got somebody that wanna talk to you."

Jordynn smiled brightly and sat up, as best she could. When I gave her the phone, she screamed, "Mommy!"

"Hi, Tutu."

"Mommy, what's wrong?"

"I miss you."

"I miss you, too, Mommy. You still hurt?"

"Yeah, baby."

I decided to walk out of the room and let them talk. She was probably tripping, too, because she was gonna miss her "Tutu's" first day of school. My mind quickly shifted back to Ashahve. I couldn't wait to see her in the morning, and I was gonna tell her everything. Shawty was gon' be sick of my ass before it was over, but I needed her, and I refused to go on without her. I knew Dr. Coleman was a rebound nigga. She was only using him to try to fill the void of not having what she needed from me. I was the one she chose.

So, I wasn't threatened by his ass, and I hoped he wasn't on that bullshit he was on before. That was the only thing that bothered me about her dipping back to that nigga. If he started doing crazy shit, like last time, I wouldn't be able to stop myself from fucking him up. As soon as I handled shit with Ashahve, I was gonna find Mali's ass. I still didn't know how she got Shavi's phone number or how she managed to take those pictures of us fucking without me noticing. I would have thrown that damn phone in the toilet.

"Da-dy!"

I went to her room to see her blowing a kiss at the screen. She smiled at me, then handed the phone to me. Piper was still there, but she looked to be drifting off to sleep. "Thank you, Rich."

"You're welcome. We'll Facetime you in the morning, when we bring Jordynn to school. Ashahve is going to be with us."

"Okay. I'm sorry. They gave me something for pain, while I was on the phone with Tutu, and this shit about to take me out."

I smiled at her. "Okay. Talk to you in the morning."

"Okay. I love you, Rich."

I smiled, not really knowing how to respond. "Aight, shawty. Get some rest."

Ms. Joyce must had slipped the phone from her, because her eyes closed before she could end the call.

⚜

I COMBED my baby girl's hair into two pigtails as she looked at me with those beautiful brown eyes. After putting a headband on her head, there was a knock at the door. My heart was beating erratically in my chest as I walked to the door. It was ten 'til seven, so it could only be Ashahve. Ms. Joyce said she would try to make it, but I didn't think she would. I checked the peephole to see Shavi standing there. When I opened the door, we stood there staring at one another for a moment. "Shavi!" Jordynn yelled, breaking us both from our trance.

"Jordynn! You look so beautiful! Who combed your hair?" Shavi asked her, walking through the door.

"Da-dy combed it!"

She kissed Jordynn's cheek, then stood straight and looked at me. "Hi, Omari."

"Hey."

Again, we stared at one another like we hadn't seen one another in months. She finally looked away and sat with Jordynn. They talked about school and Shavi was checking with her to see if I'd gotten everything she needed. I shook my head as Jordynn talked about this special eraser that she wanted and how I was mean and said no. After listening to them go back and forth, for another five minutes, I helped Jordynn to the car while Ashahve opened her own door and got in.

I was surprised she was gonna ride with me to the school. I just knew she was gonna follow me there. When I got in, Jordynn told Shavi about how she talked to her mommy and how I was gonna call her. To give me some time to talk to Shavi, I gave the phone to Jordynn, so she could Facetime Piper. Looking at Ashahve, in her leggings and asymmetrical tank top, I said, "You look nice, Shavi."

"So do you, Omari."

"Do you have time to talk to me after we leave Jordynn."

"Yeah. I have some time. I go to work at ten."

I nodded my head. She seemed so receptive today. I would definitely take advantage of the moment as soon as we got back to my place. I could hear Jordynn talking to Piper and the laughter between the two of them. I was glad we'd talked yesterday. Maybe, once Piper came home, we could repair our relationship, for Jordynn's sake. I'd have to trust her more. Trust wasn't something I gave freely, but I would have to loosen up just a bit.

After getting my baby in school, meeting the teacher and principal, Ashahve and I headed back to my apartment. When the teacher called her Jordynn's mom, she'd turned a light shade of red. Jordynn was the one who corrected the teacher. She'd said, *Shavi isn't my mom. My mama is in the hospital.* Then she held up my phone to the teacher so she could see Piper on Facetime. I'd chuckled at her way of setting the teacher straight.

When we got back to my apartment, I opened the door for Shavi and grabbed her hand to help her from the car. She smiled softly at me. We'd been quiet the whole drive. I was nervous about everything I had to tell her. No one knew everything about me, except one woman. She was now deceased. *Lenora Watkins.* I continued holding her hand until we got to the door. After unlocking it, I allowed Shavi to walk in first, then closed and locked the door behind us. "You hungry, Shavi?"

"No. I stopped to Dunkin Donuts earlier."

"Okay."

She sat on the couch and I followed, sitting next to her. Grabbing her hand and holding it in mine, I brought it to my lips and kissed it. This shit was harder than I thought it would be. I knew it would be hard, but shit, I underestimated this tremendously. Shavi stared at me for a moment, then put her hand to my cheek. "Omari, I'm here to listen, not judge you. You don't have to be nervous with me."

I took a deep breath and exhaled slowly. "After the events of the past two weeks, I knew that I needed to talk to you now. I don't wanna lose you, despite what my actions might have said. It's not that I fear your judgement. I fear verbalizing things that only my mama knew about me. You are the only person that has gotten close enough for me to even consider baring all."

I shifted on the sofa, to where she couldn't look directly in my face, and continued. "When I was about five years old was when I noticed that other kids had dads. I remember coming home from kindergarten, one day, and asking my mama why I didn't have a daddy. I mean, I've never met the nigga. She wouldn't even tell me his name because she said he didn't want to be a part of my life. We went round and round about that shit. I felt like I had a right to know who the bastard was. So, when Jordynn came along, I tried to provide for her everything I was missing in a father. Things he should have taught me, I had to learn on my own."

Closing my eyes, I continued. "I started hitting the streets with my cousin, when I was fourteen, trying to make money for us. It was a common occurrence for our lights to get turned off. I only did that for a couple months before my mama found out. She beat my ass within an inch of my fucking life. She said she'd sleep under a bridge before she allowed me to bring that shit in her house. Her mother had been a drug addict, when she was growing up. So, she'd done her best not to choose the same path. After she got me back on the right track, and I was about to graduate from high school, she took me to the recruiting office and made me sign up. She said Beaumont ain't had shit for me, so I needed to get out of here, before I ended up like my cousin."

Ashahve was still staring at me, attentively, as I got to one of the hardest parts of the conversation. My time in the military was pivotal in my emotional decline. It numbed me to a lot of things, and I felt unsure of how to live my life outside of the military. "Shavi, I've never spoken to you about my time in the Marines. I think that's where most of my issues stem from."

"I'm here for you. Take your time. If I need to call in, I will."

I swallowed back my emotion at her words. I felt all soft and shit. Straightening my posture, I began. "My problems didn't come until I had to do a couple of tours in Iraq. Street shit ain't got shit on war. I saw some shit that I will never forget. Killing people had become a norm for me, because you didn't know who to trust, and that included women and children. Images of dead bodies plague me at times, especially when my emotions are out of control. My last tour, I got shot in the leg. That's not my swag. It's a limp."

I watched her eyes widen. I'd never told her that I was shot. She just thought I chose not to re-enlist. I was supposed to be enlisted for six years, but I'd only done four. "It was a kid that shot me. Had I not killed him, he would've killed me. He was on his way to the ground when he shot me in the leg."

She scooted closer to me, as my body trembled. "When I got

home, my mama knew I wasn't the same Omari that had left. It was like I didn't care about nothing. I started drinking, to kind of dull the pain. Then, I started smoking weed and hanging out with niggas that didn't want nothing out of life. That's how I met Piper. One of the niggas I was hanging with was her cousin. We'd been fucking around for like six or seven months, when she told me she was pregnant. I always wore a condom, but somehow, she got pregnant anyway."

"Are you sure you were the only one she was sleeping with?" Shavi asked, finally breaking her silence.

"No and we never did a DNA test, but I knew that little girl was mine, the moment I looked at her. Although to me, she looked like Piper, she had my eyes and her fingers and toes looked like mine. As I held her in my arms, I knew I had to do better. I had to be a better man and whether she was biologically mine or not, she'd saved my life. I couldn't let her go. So, I never asked for a DNA test, and I'm surely not getting one now."

"I wouldn't expect you to, now. She's been your baby for four years. Like you said, regardless of her blood type, she's yours."

I nodded in agreement, as thoughts of Lenora Watkins filled my mind. We'd never really talked about my mama. She'd come to the cemetery with me and I knew that Shavi knew how much my mama meant to me, but to actually verbalize how much I loved her always caused an overabundance of emotions to fill my insides and threaten to spill out in the form of tears. Noticing it was almost nine, I let out an exasperated breath.

Ashahve noticed my reaction. She took out her cell phone and called her job. I could hear her boss getting an attitude with her, saying that she'd just come back to work after taking a week off. I grabbed her hand and shook my head. "Go to work, shawty," I whispered.

She stared at me, then said in the receiver, "I quit, then."

My eyebrows shot up. I didn't know what she'd seen in my eyes to make her do that. She ended the call and looked back at me. "Omari, you need me right now, and nothing is gonna come in the way of that. My parents will help me until I can get something else."

"Naw, shawty. I'm gon' help you. I can't believe you just did that shit."

"Well, I don't have a car note and I'm on my parents' insurance. I only pay for gas and my cell phone. Everything else isn't necessary. I can do my own hair and eyebrows."

"Don't worry. I got'chu."

"No. You don't have to do that."

"Listen. I know we aren't together anymore. But I know you still love me. Whether you take me back or not, I got'chu. You know why?" I didn't wait for her to respond before I answered my own question. "Because I love you, too."

I could see the moisture fill her eyes, as she nodded. Looking away from her, I tried to prepare my heart for the pending conversation topic. Soon after, I realized there was nothing I could do to prepare myself. I looked back at Ashahve and began again. "About six months after Jordynn was born, I came home to find my mama passed out on the floor. She'd never been sick, as far as I knew, so that shit terrified me. Not knowing my daddy, all I had were my aunt and her punk ass son. My grandparents were both deceased, and both of their families were from somewhere in Louisiana that we never visited."

I was trembling and about to lose my shit. Ashahve could tell. She put her hands to my cheeks and pulled me to her. I kissed her long and until I felt a little more relaxed. This shit was bothering the fuck out of me. So much so, until I wasn't even hard. Everything about Ashahve Glasper turned me on... just not now. However, her display of love, understanding and compassion calmed me.

"When I got to the hospital, the doctor told me that my mama's breast cancer had metastasized. That was the first time I'd heard of her having cancer at all. He told me that he only gave her another three months. I couldn't handle that shit. I broke down in that hospital and tore all kind of shit up. That was my mama. The woman that gave birth to me, alone, in her bedroom. Her sister, whom she lived with, at the time, found her and called an ambulance. This was the same woman that worked three jobs to provide for me. She never wanted to be on the system, but eventually succumbed to food stamps, so I wouldn't go hungry."

A tear had escaped my eye and Ashahve quickly wiped it. This shit was hard, but I knew I needed to finish getting it out. "I got teased, so much, at school for not wearing the name brand clothes and being on free lunch. I started fighting to cope. My mama came to that school and whooped my ass right in the principal's office. While she was angry with me, she refused to humiliate me in front of the kids and giving them something further to tease me about. She loved me so much, she wouldn't even bring a man home. She said that I was her main priority and her love life had to wait."

By this time, the tears were falling, one behind the other. I was no longer trying to hold them back. If anybody had to see me this way, Ashahve was the only person I didn't mind seeing it. "So, to find out this amazing woman, who had put my needs before hers my whole life, was being taken away from me was devastating. I sat on the hospital floor, all night, waiting for her to wake up. When she finally did, I was so angry with her for not telling me. They sent her home, on hospice, and I got to watch my mama deteriorate right before my eyes. She was the one that made me register for school, so I could make a better life for Jordynn."

"Omari, it's killing me to see you this broken, but I see why now. Hearing how close the two of you were and that she was the only person in your life that meant as much to you is devastating to me and I didn't know her."

I nodded my head and wiped my face. "We got even closer, though. She ended up living another six months and, until the last week she was here, we talked, laughed and just spent every waking moment together. She prayed for me all the time."

"You think maybe you should seek counseling?"

"Yeah. I've been looking up psychiatrists. I could always go through the VA, too. Losing someone I love sends me on the war path. So, when Piper took Jordynn, it was like my mama dying all over again."

"I understand."

She pulled me in her arms, and I laid on her lap, while she stroked the back of my head. I felt so much better after talking to her, so hopefully, I could further open up to someone else that could help me learn to deal with my emotions in a positive manner.

❦ 20 ❦

A shahve

IT HAD BEEN a whole two weeks since Omari's meltdown. I didn't know how he was holding all that shit under wraps like that. We'd talked the whole day and went to get Jordynn from school together. She was excited to tell us about her day and we had corn dogs for dinner, one of Jordynn's favorite meals. I spent as much time as I could with Omari, when he wasn't working and took care of Jordynn for him when she got out of school, if he was at work. I hadn't told him whether we would be a couple again or not and he hadn't pressed me about it. That was on the back burner, for now. Like with Elijah, he had issues he needed to work through, first, without worrying about where we stood.

I just wanted to be there for him. He'd started counseling, last week, and when he'd come home, he went in his room and didn't come out for a couple of hours. The session had obviously pulled a lot out of him. I'd gotten Piper's phone number from him, so Jordynn could use my phone to Facetime her. Now that I knew what his underlying issues were, I did my best to understand him. He'd had one outburst, which was the day of his counseling session, but he immediately apologized. I felt horrible for him, because I couldn't imagine what it would be like to not have anyone in this world that genuinely cared for you.

I'd just finished my last class for the day and, although it was only the first day, I was ready for the shit to be over. My body wasn't used to this shit no more and I was exhausted. Every first day of school was this way, but today was worse because it was the first day of the last semester before I graduated with my bachelor's degree in sociology. I'd seen Elijah and he'd actually winked at me. That surprised me. We'd been talking at least a couple of days a week and had ended up having sex again. Why I put myself in that compromising situation again was a mystery to even me.

Omari and I hadn't had sex since that last time when he was rough with me. I didn't want to be with him, in that way, until he got used to the counseling. I couldn't be his sexual punching bag again. Shit, I wanted him so badly, though. While I'd been trying to stay away from Elijah, in that manner, I couldn't help but succumb to him. My hormones were raging and I couldn't take it any longer. Elijah seemed to understand our arrangement, and he hadn't been clingy, which was a relief.

As I walked toward my car, I saw a face that I would never forget. I wanted to approach that bitch. However, I knew I had to get to Omari's to cook dinner and to get Jordynn from school. I wasn't living there, but shit, it felt like it, as much as I was there helping out. He wouldn't be getting off until seven today. Ignoring her, I headed to the gym to turn in my registration for a new Zumba class they were starting. Once I did, I went to the restroom.

When I came out the stall, that hoe was standing in the mirror primping. I took a deep breath and washed my hands. She had to have known that I recognized her face from the pictures she'd sent me. *Mali*. Stupid bitch. I washed my hands and glanced in the mirror to see the smirk on her face. That was it. That small gesture was enough to set me off. "You got something you need to say to me?"

Her eyebrows lifted and a smile spread across her face. "I thought I said everything I needed to say when I sent the pics of your man's dick having the time of its life."

Before I could restrain myself, I popped that bitch right in her big ass mouth. She didn't know who the fuck she was playing with. I was from the hood of Port Arthur. We didn't play that shit. Just 'cause my parents had moved us to Beaumont didn't mean that shit wasn't still in me. I liked to suppress it and take the high road, but ain't no hoe was gon' disrespect me. She'd fallen back against the wall, stunned. Before she could come back at me, I popped her in her mouth again. "You got some more shit you need to say, bitch?"

She looked at the blood on her hand, then back up at me. She frowned and looked like she wanted to say something else, so I punched her in her nose. "That's for just in case you mumble to yourself about me when I walk out this bitch. Just so you know, I'm the only one Omari loves. You were just somebody to waste time with until I came back to him. Had we still been together, he wouldn't have stooped beneath me to fuck you."

I walked out that bathroom mad as hell. My hand was hurting, too. I was almost sure that it would be swollen by the time I got to Omari's. I hadn't had to fight in a long time. As I sat in my seat, I smirked to myself, then sent Omari a message. *I just fucked your girl up. Her ass better not have shit else to say, or she gon' get these hands again.*

After starting my car, I headed to his place and got started on dinner. Right after I put the lasagna in the oven, Omari called. He didn't bother texting back. "Hello?"

"What the hell you talking 'bout?"

"Hey, Omari."

"Don't hey me. What girl?"

"Mali. She had the nerve to trash talk in the bathroom, today in the gym. So, if you see her nose and mouth all fucked up, tomorrow at school, it was because I fucked her up."

"Aww, shit. That P.A. done finally showed its face. Hopefully, I won't have no classes with her ass this semester. What she said to you?"

"She was looking at me crazy, so I asked her if she had something to say. That bitch had the nerve to say she thought she said everything she needed to say when she sent the pictures of your dick having the time of his life."

"No that bitch didn't go there."

"Yeah the fuck she did."

"Damn! So, you put them hands on her? Don't make me tell Mrs. Glasper you at the school, where they spending their hard earned money, fighting."

"Shut up, Omari. Go back to work. I got some homework I wanna get a jump on."

"Bye, Rocky."

I rolled my eyes and ended the call. He thought the shit was funny. It probably was... a lil bit. After reading a couple of chapters, for an hour, I took the lasagna from the oven, then went to get Jordynn from school.

🕸️

"Are you still in love with me, Shavi?"

I looked up at him from the pan I was handwashing. Jordynn had gone to bed already, and I would be leaving as soon as I finished cleaning the kitchen. Omari gently stroked my cheek, as he patiently awaited my answer. Lowering my head, thinking about how I'd slept with Elijah again, was overwhelming. The tears fell down my cheeks and Omari lifted my head by the chin. His head tilted as he stared at me. "Why you crying? That can't be a good thing. Just be real with me, Shavi. I can handle that shit."

He stepped back, waiting for me to respond. I wiped my tears and lifted my head. "I am. I just don't know how to proceed right now."

I closed my eyes and took a deep breath. "I haven't been totally loyal to you, Omari. That's bugging the shit out of me. I'm usually better at controlling and restraining my desires."

He nodded. "We aren't a couple, though, right? I can't be mad about you fucking somebody else, can I?"

"Yeah. You can, because I would be."

He took a step closer to me. "You doing a lot of shit for me, showing me that you care. I'd be lying if I said I wasn't upset. But, had I been more open with you, once we got serious, we wouldn't be here in this mess. I guess this shit feels like déjà vu to you, huh?"

"Not quite. The first time was worse. I'm sorry, Omari. I love you, but I've been trying to keep my distance, emotionally, until you're a little more comfortable with seeing your therapist."

He nodded and walked away. Man, this shit hurt. Maybe I should distance myself from the both of them and just move on. What was it about me that I was attracted to mentally unstable men? Shit, it felt like I was unstable with all the back and forth and not being able to control my hormones. I finished washing the pan as he sat on the couch watching TV.

When I finished, I walked toward him to get my purse from the couch. There were two one-hundred-dollar bills laid on top of it. I frowned, then looked over at him. "What's this for?"

"Gas, your nails and feet and your time."

"Omari, I'm good."

I grabbed my purse and sat the money on his coffee table. My body needed a break, because my emotions and hormones were all over the damn place. I didn't know how I would do that and still be here for him. "You have to work tomorrow?"

"Naw. I'm off."

I nodded. Tomorrow, I would have to take the day to get myself together. I had two classes, then I would go home and meditate on some "nam myoho renge kyo" type of shit. As I turned to leave,

Omari stood to his feet to walk me to the door. He grabbed me by the waist and pulled me close, kissing the side of my neck. My eyes closed involuntarily. He still wanted me. That knowledge only made me sink lower. "Thank you, Ashahve, for everything. I still want us to remain friends. Can we do that?"

The tears were threatening to fall again, but I managed to suck them up. "Yeah," I said and smiled softly at him. "I probably won't come tomorrow, but I will be here Wednesday."

"Okay."

When I tried to leave, he pulled me to him and kissed my lips, allowing it to linger a bit. I closed my eyes and tried to convince myself to leave, but my feet wouldn't move. Omari stroked my cheek with his thumb. "Damn, shawty. This shit hard."

"I know."

"Then, why you doing it?"

I couldn't answer him. Opening my eyes, I kissed his lips again, then left. When I got to my car, I cried my damn eyes out.

21

E lijah

I HADN'T HEARD from Ashahve, in a few days, and I was beginning to worry about her. Since she no longer had any of my classes this semester, I rarely saw her at school. I'd texted her yesterday, just to see how she was doing, but she never responded. Nyera had been consuming a little of my time with questions about school, although I thought she was getting closer to another professor that she had to work with. Surprisingly, that didn't bother me. I'd become quite used to being alone. My sister and I had been spending almost every weekend together, when she didn't have to work.

After leaving my counseling session, I'd gone to sit with my parents for a little while. I'd been trying to do more of that lately. They were getting up in age and my dad had some issues with blockage around his heart. After the unfortunate events with Taylor, it taught me a valuable lesson. Life could be snatched away with the blink of an eye. I needed to cherish every moment I had with the ones

I loved. Not only did that include my family, it included Ashahve as well. As I sat at the traffic light, I texted her again.

You don't have to hold a conversation with me. Just let me know you're okay. I'm starting to worry.

Taking off from the light, I pulled into the gas station to get gas and run my car through the automatic carwash. Once inside the washer, Ashahve texted back. *I'm sorry. I've been sick and I still am, but I'm okay.*

She usually talked to me about what was going on with her. I couldn't dwell on it, though. If she said she was okay, then I'd have to force myself to believe that.

Once I got home, I started reading over reaction papers from my intro to sociology class. I was only teaching two this semester. Next semester, I would only be teaching one, because they would be adding another graduate class to me. Reaction papers were the students' reaction to a premise I'd given them. Basically, if they turned it in, they got an A. The papers reflected their opinions and beliefs. Those weren't gradable. However, I still liked to read them, because it helped me to teach. The papers gave me insight to my students' personalities.

Right in the middle of the last paper, my phone started to ring. I was surprised to see Nyera's number. I had spoken to her earlier today already. "Hello?"

"Have you and Ashahve fucked?"

I nearly swallowed my damn tongue. That was the last thing I was expecting her to say. "What? Why do you ask that?"

"Answer the question, Elijah."

I sighed deeply. "We did, before I even met you. When I found out y'all were cousins, I still didn't want to tell you, because I thought we had something."

"Well, y'all must have fucked recently, too. I have proof. I knew something seemed strange between the two of you, with the way you looked at one another. This is fucked up. I've been sitting on this shit for the past three weeks, because I just couldn't believe that either of you would betray me this way. After Floyd's, one of you should have said something! Especially since both of you seemed nervous as fuck!"

"I'm sorry, Nyera. Ashahve and I haven't had a relationship and it was unethical for me to be with her. So, we had to keep it a secret."

"The fucking cat is out the bag, now, isn't it? I'm about to go and confront her about this shit now."

My eyes closed as my heart ached. Nyera ended the call and I could only pray that she didn't go to the university with this. My life was just getting on the path that would lead to where I wanted it to go regarding my career. *Fuck!* I just hoped she didn't get Ashahve's parents involved in this. Rubbing my hand down my face, I called Karen. She'd been my confidant, when it came to Ashahve. "Hello?"

"Karen, I fucked up."

"What? What are you talking about?"

"Nyera somehow found out about Ashahve. Someone sent her pictures."

"Pictures? Where the hell were y'all, Eli?"

"At my house. She'd come over to talk."

"So, what did the pictures show?"

"I don't know. She just asked if I'd fucked Ashahve."

"Damn it! You probably told on yourself, Eli. The pictures may not have shown anything, or she could have been bluffing, to see what you'd say."

Fuck my life. She was right. Nyera sounded so angry, I assumed she knew. That was so damn conniving and I fell for it. "Fuck. That's what I get for trying to be honest. If she goes to the university with this, I could lose my job, Karen. I'll be done in education. I can't lose my job. I can't go back to that place in my life."

"Eli, please don't panic. I'm on my way over. Okay?"

"Okay."

I stood from my couch and started pacing. This shit was all my fault. I should've listened to Dr. Madison. Shit! Shit! Shit! I was gonna have to sell my house and move in with my parents or Karen.

My life would be over. I had to get to Nyera to stop this. Grabbing my phone from the table, I called her.

"What?"

"Nyera, I'm sorry."

"Fuck you and her."

"Nyera, we didn't mess around while you and I were together. I swear to you. We've only slept together twice since she and Omari broke up. It's not what you think."

"What do I think, since you seem to know?"

"That we have been messing around the whole time."

"That's not what I think. But I do think y'all are both under-handed, sneaky and made for each other. I hope y'all enjoy each other since it doesn't have to be a secret anymore."

She ended the call. From her words, I was hoping that she didn't go to my dean. It didn't seem like she would. My doorbell rang, so I knew it was Karen. My mind was still racing and I couldn't, for the life of me, think of who could have sent her those pictures besides Omari. Why would he do that, though? Surely, he knew that Nyera and I weren't together anymore. I opened the door to find Karen standing there with my mother. I walked away from the door, clearly in panic mode.

I felt like I was about to have an anxiety attack. My mind was telling me to put in for another job, out of town, before they found out. I needed to get away from Beaumont and just start fresh some-where else. That would be the only way to get Ashahve out of my system. Rubbing my hand down my face, my sister grabbed my arm. "Elijah, please calm down. Don't panic over the unknown. Nyera may not say anything."

My mama wrapped her arms around me. "She's right, baby. It's gonna be okay."

"I hope y'all are right. This can't happen again."

"Have you taken your medication today, already?"

"Yes, ma'am," I said, breathing deeply.

"What about your emergency stash that Dr. Madison prescribed for you when you told her you and Ashahve were messing around again?"

"I haven't taken one. I actually forgot about them," I said breathlessly.

"Okay. Where are they?"

"My nightstand. Top drawer."

After Karen took off for my room, my mama said, "Come sit down, baby."

I followed her to the couch and tried to get my breathing under control. I wondered if she'd contacted Ashahve yet? If she did, Shavi probably would have called me by now. Karen came back with my pills and gave me one from the bottle, then went to the kitchen to get me a bottle of water. My legs were trembling, uncontrollably, and hopefully that pill would kick in, sooner rather than later. Once Karen had come back with my water, I quickly downed the pill in my hand and laid my head back on the couch.

I knew that my last time with Ashahve, three weeks ago, would be my last time. Within a short time, she'd become a part of who I was. Pushing her out of my heart had been impossible and forgetting about her hadn't even been a thought. Now that I was being forced into both of those decisions, I was scared half to death.

22

Omari

"DA-DY, I can't wait to get there."

"I know. Yo' mama gon' be excited to see you."

We were on our way to Houston to visit Piper. She was still in the hospital and we'd already visited once. I didn't bother to tell her we were coming this weekend. Jordynn had wanted to surprise her. She'd drawn all kinds of pictures to hang on the wall, and I'd actually bought a plant. Although I hated therapy, the first couple of sessions had been helping me cope with everything, especially losing my mother.

I'd had to cope with losing Ashahve, too. While we had agreed to remain friends, I hadn't heard from her for the past few days. She hadn't answered her phone, nor had she returned any of my text messages. Jordynn had been asking about her, too. I'd had to scale back on my hours at work to make sure I could get to the daycare on time to pick up Jordynn. Because Ashahve and I were no longer communicating, I had to put her in the after-school program and had to have her picked up by six every day.

I'd be lying if I said I didn't miss her. Regardless of everything that had gone down, I knew she was the one for me. We fit too perfectly. I caused our downward spiral. However, I couldn't dwell on that, I was just hoping that she eventually called to let me know she was okay. Jordynn had been asking about her and I didn't know what to say. I'd even texted once to say that Jordynn wanted to Face-time her and there was still no response. Something had to be going on and, tomorrow, if I had to, I was gonna call Mrs. Glasper to find out.

When we got to the hospital, Jordynn was so excited to be spending time with Piper. The last visit went well. Piper had started having problems with blood clots, though. They had her on blood thinners to prevent any more from developing, but they were somehow forming anyway. She seemed exhausted as well. This time, we decided to come earlier in the day. Last time, we didn't get here until two.

It was tough getting Jordynn around, last time, but the nurse told me to ask for a wheelchair this time, so I didn't have to carry her the whole way. I didn't have a problem carrying my baby but, the minute Jordynn heard "wheelchair," she was ready to be pushed in one. As soon as we parked, she said, "Da-dy, don't forget to get a wheelchair."

I rolled my eyes, then got out and lifted her in my arms. She'd been my exercise for sure. When we were at home, I'd lay on the floor and lift her like she was free weights. She got a kick out of that. Although she could walk, the hospital was so huge, letting her walk would take us all day to get to Piper. Once we'd gotten inside and a nurse saw us, she immediately went to get a wheelchair. The nurse was so taken aback with Jordynn's beauty and spirit, she pushed her all the way to Piper's room.

However, before we could go in, several nurses ran by us, nearly knocking me down to get inside. Before I could panic and run inside, the nurse that had pushed Jordynn up, stopped me. "You won't be able to go in. Someone will come out and tell you what's going on."

Before I could protest, Ms. Joyce came out the room with tears streaming down her face. My heart sank to my feet and my breathing became shallow. Jordynn was sitting in the wheelchair, crying. "Momo, what happened to Mommy?"

"She was having trouble breathing, baby."

The nurse started talking to Jordynn as I kept my eyes on Ms. Joyce. "Is it okay if I take her to the playroom down the hall?"

I nodded my head while still staring at Ms. Joyce. I needed her to tell me something. Too much was going on right now. This therapist had all my fucking feelings on my sleeve, so I didn't know if I could handle too much more. Once the nurse had walked off pushing Jordynn and talking excitedly about the play area, Ms. Joyce fell into my chest. She'd been holding that in, in front of Jordynn. "She just stopped breathing and went limp. Rich, I don't know what happened. It was like she passed out."

I held her close as we stood outside the door waiting. Allowing a tear to drop, the only person I wanted there to console me was Ashahve. She was the only woman that had ever seen me weak. I closed my eyes, as I heard my baby laughing, having the time of her life while her mother was in that room fighting for hers. When the door finally opened, and I saw the crash cart come out and the long faces, I knew it was over. Ms. Joyce tried to go in the room, but the doctor held her back. "I'm so sorry. We lost her."

Ms. Joyce started screaming and I could hear Jordynn's laughter stop. "My baby! No! I can't lose my baby!"

Her knees gave out and she fell to the floor screaming. I knelt next to her and pulled her in my arms. After trying to console her for a moment, I helped her to her feet. Jordynn and I were too late. I was just glad we got to see her last weekend. We slowly walked in her room, like we were hoping that she would somehow be awake, playing a cruel joke on us, only to find her lying there with her eyes and mouth open. I bit my bottom lip to hold back the emotion, as Ms. Joyce got in bed with Piper, crying over her dead body.

As I stared at Piper, I began praying silently for God to keep me focused on my baby girl. I'd found myself praying quite a bit these days. Walking closer to Piper, I slid my hand down her face, closing her eyes, then kissed her forehead. A tear fell down my cheek and I quickly swiped it. I had to go get my baby girl. Ms. Joyce was in denial, lying next to Piper's lifeless body, talking to her like she would respond. "So, when you get all better, you are going to come live with me. I could use the help around the house. Jordynn definitely won't mind that. Then she'll get to spend time with you and me at the same time."

She stroked Piper's hair and kissed her cheek. "They said you'll be in a wheelchair for a while, because you'll have to go through therapy to learn how to walk again. You're strong, though, so that'll be a walk in the park for you."

I couldn't take any more. Listening to her talk to Piper like she was still alive was getting the best of me. I walked out the room, then slid my hand down my face, trying to compose myself before breaking the news to my baby girl. While Piper and I didn't get along, sometimes, to see the mother of my daughter lying there was hard as hell. As I went down the hallway, to the playroom, I felt my phone vibrate. Taking it from my pocket, I saw a text from Mali.

My better judgement said not to open it, because I couldn't deal with her bullshit right now. I didn't listen. I opened the message to see, *I done really fucked your ex's world up now. She gon' learn not to fuck with me.*

I rolled my eyes. That was probably why Ashahve wasn't talking to me now. I blocked Mali's number without responding and headed to my baby. When I got to the playroom, the nurse was holding her close. As I got closer to them, she lifted her head. "Da-dy, Momo was screaming. What's wrong?"

I swallowed the lump in my throat and looked at my baby girl, dreading having to tell her that her mama was dead. I searched my

mind and heart on how to explain this to her where she could understand. After sitting in the little chair, she left the nurse's lap and
limped over to mine. "You remember when we talked about heaven?"

"Yes! That's where Max went."

Max was her puppy. For her third birthday party, I'd bought it for
her. Only, a week later, he ran out into the street and got ran over by a
truck. "Yeah, baby girl."

I lowered my head, because I didn't want to see her cry. "Today,
Mommy went to meet God. So, now she's an angel."

"Mommy got hit by a truck, too. Now, she's gone?"

It didn't dawn on me that Piper and Max had met the same fate,
until she'd said so. "Yeah, baby girl."

She started crying and hugged my neck, laying her head on my
shoulder. Hearing her whimpers did nothing to alleviate my pain.
The tears rolled down my cheeks as I tried to console my baby and
prepare her to live the rest of her life without her mother.

⚜

I PULLED my tie from around my neck and laid on the couch. I'd just
gotten home from Piper's funeral. It had been a whole week since
she'd died. The doctors thought that she'd suffered from a blood clot
traveling to her heart but, to be sure, they were having an autopsy
done. Ms. Joyce had asked for Jordynn to stay with her tonight and I
agreed to it. Visitors had kept her busy, during the week, but now that
the funeral was over, people were going back to their regular lives,
leaving Ms. Joyce to continue to cope alone. Although Piper's death
hurt me, I knew what I felt didn't scratch the surface of what Ms.
Joyce felt.

After pulling my shoes off, there was a knock at the door. I sighed
deeply, wondering who was showing up at my crib unannounced.
Looking through the peephole, my body temperature skyrocketed. It
was Ashahve. I hadn't talked to her in over three weeks. I didn't text
her to let her know that Piper had died. She hadn't been responding

to text messages or answering calls, so I'd given up. When I opened the door, she stood there in some blue jeans and a t-shirt.

Her eyes had sadness in them, and it looked like she'd been crying. While I wanted to pick her up and hug her tightly, I decided to play it cool. "What's up, shawty?"

She glanced behind me, probably looking for Jordynn. "Um... my parents still get the newspaper. When Mama saw Piper's face, she started screaming, thinking about Jordynn and how hard this has to be for her. How is she?"

"She's okay."

"I'm sorry to show up without calling first. I just wanted to check on her."

She turned to walk away, as I stood there allowing my heart to go to war with my mind. My heart was saying don't let her leave, but my mind was saying if she gave a damn about you, she would have called in those three weeks you hadn't heard from her. She looked like life was getting the best of her, and all I wanted to do was hold her in my arms. "Shavi!"

She stopped walking and turned to face me. I walked to her and grabbed her hand, leading her back to my apartment. After closing the door, I asked, "What's been up wit'chu?"

She only shook her head. Why didn't she want to talk to me? "Shavi, you can talk to me. You know that."

She lowered her face to her hands for a moment, then said, "I didn't come here to talk about me. How are you handling this?"

"Shavi..."

"No. How are you, Omari?"

"I'm okay. It's hard, but I'm dealing with it."

She nodded. We sat there quietly for a moment. "Where's Jordynn?"

"She with Ms. Joyce."

"Okay. Tell her I came by to check on her. I have to go."

"Shavi, for real? You not gon' tell me what's up?"

Whatever was on her mind had to be heavy. When I saw the

tears, I went and sat next to her and grabbed her hand. Damn, I still loved her, and seeing her this way was only making me worry more. Her hand was trembling as she tried to compose herself. Once she looked in my eyes, she said, "Nyera knows about me and Dr. Coleman. She threatened to go to the dean. I worked hard for my grades. I earned them. If they strip my credits from me, I don't know what I'm gonna do."

"Why would they strip your credits?"

"If she tells the college we had an affair, they're gonna think that he gave me those grades. I worked my ass off. I didn't need special favors."

"Damn. How did she find out?"

"I don't know."

Mali's text message from last week came to mind, but how did she know about Shavi and Dr. Coleman? I suppose the same way she got Shavi's phone number. "If you need someone to vouch for your character, you know I'm here."

"No. I can't let you do that. I've hurt you enough. I shouldn't even be telling you this. I have to go."

She stood from the couch and quickly made her way to the door, as I followed behind her. "It was good to see you, Omari."

"It was good to see you, too."

After opening the apartment door, she practically ran to her car. When she got to it, she ducked inside without even looking back, as I stood there watching her leave.

23

A shahve

"So, you just gon' sit there and act like you don't know what I'm talking about?"

"Nyera..."

"No, fuck you, Shavi. You are my cousin. When you saw me dating a man you were sleeping with, you should've told me."

We'd met at Riverfront Park to talk. She'd called me for the first time, in weeks, and said there was something important she needed to talk to me about. She obviously knew more than I was willing to admit. I'd been quiet. She, then, took her cell phone out and showed me pictures of my car at his house. She'd been following me. The pictures were from the last time I was there. Finally giving in, I said, "How was I supposed to tell you something nobody was supposed to know? Nyera, he and I had to keep what we did a secret. I earned every grade I got, and I didn't want anyone to question that."

"Well, it definitely looks shady. You fucking your professor and you happen to get all As in his class."

"I got A's in other classes, too."

"Shit, maybe they need to see if you fucking other professors then."

I stopped trying to explain, because I was ready to beat her ass now. To call me a cheater and an opportunist was blowing me. I'd graduated at the top of my class in high school and had been getting A's in college long before I made my infatuation with Dr. Coleman known to him. She left me sitting there, on the bench, wondering if my career was over before it started.

That entire conversation with Nyera had made me sick... literally. Immediately afterwards, I had to run to the restroom and throw up. And, now, two weeks later, I was still worried sick. There had been no word of either of us being called to the carpet, so I was hopeful that she didn't report our affair. I hadn't seen her since, and I'd only seen Elijah once at school. I'd actually missed a couple of days after that. I was still scared to death, but I knew I had to go to class. Proof of how I was doing in other classes, besides his, should be a testament to how knowledgeable I was and how much I studied.

I was also worried about Elijah and his mental state. If he lost his job, it would kill him. He wouldn't be able to get another job teaching. Him being jobless again scared me. How he sank into a deep depression after Taylor ran game on him, then again when she got killed, led me to believe that if anything else, of that magnitude, happened again, he would be successful in his attempt to kill himself. He would make sure of it. That thought alone scared me more than anything.

As if I wasn't worried enough, the focus of my worry shifted from me and Elijah to Jordynn and Omari. I'd been avoiding him because of the shit Nyera had on my mind. I didn't want to have him worrying about me. Even though he already knew about me and Dr. Coleman, I had no desire to involve him in my three-act drama. But when my mama showed me Piper's obituary in the paper, I cried. Just imagining what they were going through made me get in my car to go see about them. Omari looked like he was doing well and that made me happy.

After I left his apartment and had gotten back home, I went to my room and laid down. Once I'd been there for an hour or so, someone knocked on my door. "Come in."

When the door cracked open, I saw my mama standing there. She peeked her head in and smiled at me. "Hey, baby. Have you still been feeling sick?"

"Yes, ma'am. My appetite is non-existent and I'm always tired."

She walked in, holding a bag. I frowned slightly, as she smiled big. "What's that?"

"It's a pregnancy test. I've been watching you for the past month. You haven't had a cycle, Shavi, and you're exhibiting all the symptoms consistent with pregnancy."

I'd been hoping the symptoms would go away, because, in the back of my mind, I felt like I was pregnant. Omari and I had stopped using condoms a long time ago, but I'd missed a couple of pills. Elijah and I had only slept together twice, but the problem was that we didn't use condoms either. I was so stupid. Missing those couple of pills could have me raising a kid before I wanted to. There was no way I'd be able to start graduate school, next semester, if I was pregnant.

I wouldn't know who the baby was for. My mama was beaming because she's been begging for a grandbaby, hence the reason she attached to Jordynn so quickly. She also assumed the baby was for Omari. If I told her that I didn't know who the baby was for, she would want to kill me. So, I was hoping like hell that I wasn't. My period was late, but I'd skipped a month before.

"Mama..."

"No, ma'am. Get up and take this test."

I threw the covers off me, then almost snatched the bag from her. "Alright, li'l girl. You ain't too old to get that ass popped."

I headed to the bathroom, while rolling my eyes where she couldn't see me. My mama wasn't about to hem me up in here. When

I got inside and began opening the box, my hands were trembling and my heart was racing. My mind was going ninety to nothing as well. "Please, don't let me be pregnant," I said aloud to myself.

After reading the instructions, I sat on the toilet and started pissing, then put the tip of the test in the stream. Once I pulled it out, I put the cap on the tip and wiped it down with a piece of toilet paper. I sat the test on the countertop, but I couldn't move after that. My entire body was shaking like a leaf. I could barely focus enough to wipe, flush and pull my pants up.

Washing my hands took forever, because I was trying not to look at that test. However, I knew it was time to put myself out of my misery. Just as I was about to look at the test, my mama knocked on the door. "Shavi, hurry up!" she said excitedly.

She was feeling the total opposite of what I felt. I closed my eyes and picked up the test from the countertop. It was one of those digital tests. There was no confusing what it would read. If I was pregnant, it would read "pregnant," but if I wasn't, it would say, "not pregnant." So, here was the moment of truth. I slowly opened my eyes to see the black letters spelled out across the small screen. *Pregnant.*

To Be Continued...

AFTERWORD

From the Author

I hope you enjoyed part two of this story! Don't try to come for me because of how it ended. LOL Book three will be available before you know it! I really appreciate you taking this journey with me. There's also a great playlist on iTunes for this book under the same title. Please keep up with me on Facebook (@authormonicawalters), Instagram (@authormonicawalters), and Twitter (@monlwalters). You can also visit my Amazon author page at www.amazon.com/author/monica.walters to view my releases. For live discussions, give-aways, and inside information on upcoming releases, join my Facebook group, Monica's Romantic Sweet Spot at https://bit.ly/2P2lo6X.

Ultimatum: #lovemeorleaveme, Part 2

CPSIA information can be obtained
at www.ICGtesting.com
Printed in the USA
LVHW111450011119
636084LV00003B/421/P